Susan's shoulders slumped.

She looked like she felt—tired. People probably thought she was Lewis's agent or business manager. Certainly not his girlfriend. Correction, fake girlfriend.

What made Lewis think the idea would work? No way, people wouldn't believe they were an item.

All her life, she wondered what it would be like to fit. To feel accepted by someone. Anyone. She had a lot to offer, if people would only look.

Don't be so dramatic, her mother would say. *People don't look if there's nothing to look at.*

Lewis Matola was offering people something to look at.

Would it be so horrible if the world saw her as someone different? Just for a little while?

Rummaging through her bag, she located a hair tie and forced her curls into a messy bun. Then, she shed her jacket. The black turtleneck wasn't stylish, but at least the world could see she had a waist.

Lewis was biting into his sandwich when she returned. She tossed her bag on the bench and slid in next to him. "You've got a deal."

Dear Reader,

How many of us have felt like we didn't fit in?

As soon as Susan Collier told off the heroine in *Her Christmas Miracle*, I knew she needed a love story of her own. For all her tough talk, Susan is the misfit of the Collier family. I couldn't wait to find a hero for her and soften those sharp edges.

A woman as strong-minded as Susan needs a strong partner. Enter Lewis Matola, former bad boy footballer. (That's soccer for my American readers.) Lewis is a misfit, too, and in his case, has compounded his problem by developing a sordid reputation.

Both of them think that they could use an image makeover. What they really need is someone to love them unconditionally.

I loved writing Lewis and Susan's faux romance. The fact that my editor asked me to set the story at Christmastime made their pretend dates so much fun to write. There's nothing like romance amid the snowflakes and holiday lights. There's a touch of magic in the air this time of season.

Please let me know what you think of this story at Barbara@BarbaraWallace.com.

Love,

Barbara

Her Convenient Christmas Date

Barbara Wallace

H HARLEQUIN® ROMANCE

Recycling programs
for this product may
not exist in your area.

ISBN-13: 978-1-335-49960-8

Her Convenient Christmas Date

First North American publication 2019

Copyright © 2019 by Barbara Wallace

Printed in U.S.A.

Barbara Wallace can't remember when she wasn't dreaming up love stories in her head, so writing romances for Harlequin Romance is a dream come true. Happily married to her own Prince Charming, she lives in New England with a house full of empty-nest animals. Occasionally her son comes home, as well! To stay up-to-date on Barbara's news and releases, sign up for her newsletter at barbarawallace.com.

Books by Barbara Wallace

Harlequin Romance

Visit the Author Profile page
at Harlequin.com for more titles.

To all the square pegs in the world.
May we love our edges.

Praise for
Barbara Wallace

CHAPTER ONE

THE BAR WAS one of those pop-up, themed locations that were trendy at the moment. Holiday Cheer was the name and its existence had temporarily transformed the mezzanine of the Regis Hotel into a garish, yet strangely enticing Christmas wonderland. The walls were made entirely of poinsettia blossoms, while strings of holiday lights crisscrossed the air like tiny multicolored stars.

In the middle of the cheer, at a bar framed by Christmas trees, Susan Collier was having a deep, meaningful conversation with her cocktail glass.

"So what if I don't have a date? It's not like I have the plague. Plenty of women go to weddings without a plus-one."

Her cocktail, the sympathetic ear that it was, didn't disagree.

Too bad Ginger and Courtney weren't as

sympathetic. The two catty little trolls from marketing enjoyed a good laugh about her while powdering their noses. So good, in fact, they didn't realize Susan was in the stall listening to every word.

"Is it any wonder?" one of them had said. "She's got a perpetual stick up her bum. I don't know why Maria invited her to the wedding in the first place."

"I should fire them both for insubordination," Susan muttered. The cocktail offered itself up in mute solidarity. Lifting the glass, she polished off the contents in one swallow.

"You're drinking those pretty quickly. Sure you don't want to slow down?" the bartender asked when she signaled for another.

"Didn't realize there was a speed limit." She tapped the rim of her empty glass with her index finger. "Keep 'em coming. And, if you're worried about me toddling off and driving, don't. I used a car service." Because that was what women without dates did. They car serviced.

"Aren't you afraid they'll miss you upstairs?"

Susan snorted. Did he mean the wedding to which she'd received an obligatory invitation just because her office was next to the bride's? The one for which she had stuffed herself into shapeware and a vintage dress with the hopes it would make her Kardashianesque rear end look its best? Doubtful.

"Just make the drink," she told him.

"All right. But don't say I didn't warn you," the man replied.

Warning taken. Whatever the warning was.

She didn't know why she'd bothered attending this wedding in the first place. If Maria Borromeo hadn't been one of the few people who was moderately friendly toward her, Susan would have canceled when her brother Linus backed out of being her date. No one would have cared then any more than they would care if she spent the entire reception sucking back gin cocktails in the bar.

She knew her reputation. *Shrewsan*, they called her when they didn't think she was listening. It was no secret she was the least popular Collier at Collier's Soap. Her brothers—half brothers, that is—inherited all the positive Collier traits. Things like the Collier charm and lanky athletic good looks. She, on the other hand, didn't get the Collier anything. Nor did she get any of the good Quinn characteristics either, as her mother used to love pointing out. Except perhaps a passing resemblance to a great-aunt Ruth, the dumpy one.

The bartender returned with another red cocktail with an extra cherry this time. Susan forgave him for his earlier question. He was a good guy, Mr. Bartender. She liked how his red flannel shirt and neat white beard matched the Christmas decor.

"What do you call this thing anyway?" she asked him when he set the drink down. The cocktail list had been full of cute holiday-themed names that she hadn't bothered to read, zeroing in on the first one that listed gin instead.

"A Christmas Wish," he replied. "Guaranteed to make your wishes come true."

Susan barked out a laugh. "You mean if I drink enough of these I'll meet Prince Charming?"

"Is that what you want?"

"Hardly." Clearly he wasn't as good a listener as her cocktail friend. Cinderella Complexes were for the Gingers and Courtneys of the world. She was rich and successful in her own right, and her half brothers weren't wicked. "I'm not waiting for some man to rush in and rescue me from my miserable existence."

Although every once in a while…

She stared deep into the contents of the glass where tiny bubbles rose from the bottom. Every once in a while she wished there was someone who really understood her. Her brothers…they loved her, but great as they were, they didn't really "get" her. They didn't understand what it was like to be the perpetual square peg in a round hole, always pretending she fit.

How lovely it would be to share her life with someone who saw the truth. With whom she could fit without having to pretend. Who thought her beautiful and special, warts and all.

She was getting maudlin. And the room was spinning. Maybe the bartender was right and she'd had enough. Why else would she be wishing for things that weren't ever going to happen?

"Hey, mate, do me a favor and get me a glass of soda water, will you?"

A tall, perfectly carved physical specimen of a man approached the bar, his face dripping wet. From the red stain on his shirt collar, Susan guessed he'd been the recipient of a Christmas Wish square in the face.

"Word of advice," he said to the bartender,

his words coated in a Yorkshire accent. "Before you agree to be in a wedding, make sure you haven't hooked up with anyone on the guest list."

"Ran into a bitter ex-girlfriend, did you?"

"Two. And they compared notes." He grabbed a stack of cocktail napkins and began wiping the liquid from his face.

"Must have been *some* notes," she muttered.

He looked in her direction for the first time. "You're not going to lob your drink at me too, are you?"

"Why would I do that?"

"I dunno. Female solidarity or something. You're here for Hank and Maria's wedding, right? For all I know, they're your friends too."

"That would require me to have friends." Had she said that out loud?

He arched his brow in a mixture of half surprise, half curiosity. Oh, well, too late to take the comment back now. Besides, it was the truth. She didn't have friends. She had family, she had colleagues and she had acquaintances, but friends? That would involve allowing people closer than arm's length, an impossible task when you were a square peg.

It was hard enough trying to pretend your edges didn't matter.

"Sounds like I'm not the only one who got burned tonight. Weddings aren't the fun people make them out to be, are they? Unless you're the bride and groom, that is, and even then... Thanks, mate."

The bartender had returned with the soda water along with a white cloth napkin. "No problem. I don't suppose I can get an autograph when you finish? I'm a huge fan. That stop you made against Germany a few years ago? I've never seen anything like it."

"Thanks. Definitely a finer moment than this one."

Ah. Susan recognized him now. This was the infamous Lewis Matolo. Maria mentioned her fiancé knew the former footballer. She'd been in a downright tizzy over his attendance at the wedding. Matolo, or "Champagne Lewis" as the tabloids called him, came with a reputation. Then again, if your nickname involved alcohol, that was probably a given. He'd gotten the moniker after they snapped his picture leaving a London nightclub, shirtless, with a woman under each arm and an open bottle of Cristal in each hand.

From what Susan had read, it wasn't an unusual occurrence.

She watched as he dipped a corner into the glass and began dabbing at a red spot on the front of his shirt. Sadly, he didn't succeed in doing anything more than turning the spot into a damp pink stain.

"You're going to need detergent," Susan told him. "Otherwise, all you're doing is making it worse."

He looked up through his long lashes. "Are you sure?"

"I own a soap company. Trust me." Scented soaps and moisturizers hardly made her an expert. More like she tended to dribble food down her front. But being a soap mogul sounded better.

"You own a... Oh, you're Maria's boss. Hank mentioned you."

Oh, good. That made two of them whose reputations preceded them. "Susan Collier, at your service," she said, saluting him with her glass.

He nodded, apparently assuming it wasn't necessary to offer a name in return. "So what's got you holed up avoiding the good times in the ballroom, Susan Collier? Shouldn't you be upstairs dancing with your date?"

"I didn't come with a date."

"Sorry."

Not him too. Why was everyone suddenly sorry for her dating status all of a sudden? "For your information, I could get a date if I wanted one. I chose not to. A woman is not defined by her dating record."

She tried to punctuate her statement with a wave of her arm only to come dangerously close to needing her own damp cloth. To make amends for her clumsiness, she took a healthy sip. These drinks were delicious.

"Again, okay. I only meant sorry for presuming. Didn't mean to touch a nerve." Hands up in appeasement, he backed a few inches away.

From his place a few feet down the bar, the bartender chuckled. "Maybe you should quit while you're ahead, mate."

"No kidding. Tonight's definitely not my night," he said as he strained to look down at his shirt. "You're right. Made it worse, didn't I?"

"Told you," Susan replied. "It's the grenadine. Stuff's impossible to get out. Tastes good though."

"I'll take your word for it. Damn. Now I'm

going to smell like a fruit bowl for the rest of the night."

"I hate to ask, but what did you do to earn a cocktail to the face in the first place?"

A better question would have been what didn't he do? Lewis tossed the napkin on the bar. He'd been drowning in the karma from a decade of bad decisions for the past nine months. "Nothing," he lied. "One minute we were talking, the next I had a maraschino cherry in my hair."

"Just like that?"

"Yeah, just like that."

She knew he was lying. It was evident from the look she shot him over the rim of her glass.

"You're leaving something out," she said. "I can tell by the way you're not saying anything."

"What?"

"You heard me." She was swaying on her bar stool, the way someone did when the room was starting to spin. Hopefully the bartender was paying attention. "People don't toss perfectly good drinks for no reason," she said. "*Especially* good drinks. So what did you do?"

It was none of her business, Lewis wanted to say, except the glint in her eye made him bite his tongue. Even drunk, she had an astuteness about her.

What the heck. She'd hear anyway. "I might have asked them for their names."

"You forgot who they were? Both of them? After you slept with them?"

He didn't say he was proud of it. In fact, he was horrified. "They were from my playing days," he replied.

"Oh, why didn't you say so? They were from his playing days," she announced to the bartender. "That totally makes it all right."

"I didn't say it was right. Just that's why I forgot them." He was lucky he remembered his playing days at all.

"I completely understand. It must have been hard keeping all those groupies straight."

Yes, it was, because there had been a lot of groupies and a lot of alcohol and they were all a giant blur of bad behavior. Lewis kept his mouth shut, however, because it was no excuse. Besides, the woman was drunk and he knew from experience that alcohol and arguing didn't mix. "Are you always this sarcastic to people you just met?" he asked.

"Meh. Depends on how easy a target."

"You're saying I'm easy."

She eyed him through her lashes. "You tell me, Champagne."

How he hated that name. If he never heard the nickname again, it wouldn't be soon enough. The irony of the situation—if that was the right word—was that he didn't remember the picture being taken.

"I'm beginning to see why you don't have friends."

His companion's lower lip started to tremble.

Terrific. On top of everything, he'd gone and hurt her feelings. Why not stomp on a puppy for an encore? "You're not going to cry, are you?"

She responded with a sniff. "Don't be silly. I don't cry."

She was doing a darn good impression of tearing up. Lewis handed her one of the cocktail napkins from his pile. "Here, dry your eyes."

"I told you. I'm not going to cry."

"Then wipe your nontears with it before they make your mascara run," he said. "And, I'm sorry. The comment was uncalled for."

"Yes, it was. It's also true."

"I'm sure it's…"

"I'm in a bar getting drunk by myself and no one from upstairs has noticed I'm missing."

"I'm sure someone has noticed," Lewis replied. Granted, she wasn't the kind of girl he'd look for, but she was hardly forgettable. Her black dress was sexy in a naughty-secretary way—prim but tight enough to show she had curves. She had black curly hair that she'd pulled into a high ponytail—to match the dress he presumed. It worked together to give her a no-nonsense vibe. If there was such a thing as a no-nonsense sex kitten, she was it.

"If it helps, no one's looking for me either," he said.

"Of course they aren't," she said, dabbing her eyes. "You insulted two women."

"And here I'd gone five whole minutes without thinking of my stupidity." Good to know her tears didn't dull the bite of her tongue.

"Now you know why no one's looking for me, except my friend here." She waved her half-empty martini glass, the red liquid sloshing against the sides. "Unless you want your reputation to get worse, you might want to slide down a few stools."

"Trust me, my reputation can't get much worse, luv." A drink in the face was nothing when everyone in the UK thought you were washed up. Maybe not everyone, he corrected, but the people who counted. Like the people at BBC Sport who thought Pete "White Noise" Brockton made a good commentator.

"More likely, you're going to mess up your reputation sitting with me," he told her.

"Whatever. Here's to our rotten reputations. Oh, no!" The liquid had splashed over the rim when she'd waved her drink. Running down the stem, it dripped onto the napkin he'd tossed down earlier. "And she'd been such a good friend."

Her lip was wobbling again. Reaching into her space, he took the glass from her hand before she could take another sip.

"Hey! What are you doing?"

"I think you've had enough." Personified drinks were never a good sign. From out of the corner of his eye, he saw the bartender hold up four fingers.

"Why does everyone keep saying that?" She went to grab the drink only to pitch forward. Fortunately, her hand grabbed the bar rail, keeping her from falling completely.

Without missing a beat, she continued. "It's Christmastime. A girl should get as many wishes as she wants."

"Christmas Wishes," the bartender supplied when Lewis frowned. "It's the name of the drink."

"Well, you're going to wish you didn't have this last wish tomorrow morning. Why don't we switch to water for a little while? Get you hydrated."

"I don't need water. I'm fine."

"Trust me." Lewis set the drink on the bar as far down as he could reach. If she wanted it, she was going to have to stand up and walk around him. "You're an expert on soap? I'm an expert on getting drunk. You need water."

"Fine. I'll have the water." The way she huffed and rolled her eyes like a teenager proved his point. Lewis had a feeling she wouldn't be caught dead making such an expression sober.

"Thank you. Bartender?"

Giving a nod, the bearded man poured two large glasses, minus ice. "Room temperature will go down a little easier," he said.

Good man. Lewis took the fuller of the two glasses and handed it to Susan. "Here, drink up. Then I'll call a car to take us home. You'll have to pick up your car in the morning."

"Don't have one," she said in between swallows. "Took a car service."

"Even better."

"Wait a second. You're taking me home?" She looked up at him through her lashes.

Wow. Her eyes were really pretty. He wasn't sure if it was the sheen from the tears or the bar lighting but the hazel color had a copper center that looked lit from within. They were almost hypnotic.

"I'm making sure you get home safely," he told her. While he imagined she could handle herself, Lewis didn't like the idea of sending her home alone—car service or not. "We'll share a ride and I'll have the driver drop you off first."

"Oh." Her gaze dropped to her glass. "That's very nice of you."

There was no missing the disappointment in her voice. He didn't stop to think, but after going on about no one liking her, his dropping her off was probably a kick in the teeth. When she sobered up, she'd be really embarrassed.

"Bad form to leave a woman alone when she's been drinking," he said. "Or, to take advantage of her." Not that he would have taken her home, but he might as well take the sting out of his rejection.

It worked. A tiny blush bloomed in her cheeks. "You're a very decent person," she said. "Even if you did forget those women's names."

Lewis couldn't remember the last time he was called decent. "Thank you. If you get a chance, spread the word. I'm in need of an image makeover." A big one. Otherwise, he'd be stuck as "Champagne Lewis" for the rest of his life. Or worse, he'd fade into obscurity.

"You and me both," she replied.

"Amen to that, sister." Helping himself to the other water, he clinked the bottom of his glass against hers. "Amen to that."

CHAPTER TWO

IF THERE WERE two things Susan detested, they were headaches and people bothering her when she wanted to be left alone. Saturday morning brought both: a blinding headache and a phone ringing loudly right next to her ear.

Lifting her head from the sofa—where she'd collapsed facedown after stumbling from the bathroom—she glared at the caller ID, planning on killing the person.

Just her luck, it was her brother Thomas. One of two people in the UK she couldn't kill. He was also the only person whose call she had to take. As CEO of Collier's, he was technically her boss.

That didn't mean she had to be pleasant though. "Do you know what time it is?" she growled.

"Happy Saturday to you, as well. It's ten o'clock in the morning."

Really? She pulled the phone from her ear to check. When she'd lain down, it was just before seven that day. "Sorry. Thought it was earlier."

It suddenly dawned on her why Thomas could be calling. "Rosalind didn't have the baby, did she?" She pushed herself upright, ignoring how the blood rush made the room—and her stomach—sway.

"Not yet. The doctor thinks she'll go right on her due date, same as she did with Maddie. And you sound like dirt."

She felt like dirt. No longer having to worry about being alert, she slid down into the cushions. "Maria's wedding was last night. I overdosed on sloe gin."

"Sounds like a good time."

"Not as good as you'd think." And ending with her nearly falling on her face when she tripped going up her front steps—right after she'd insisted she was perfectly able to navigate the walk on her own. She could just imagine the look that had crossed Lewis Matolo's face when he caught her by the waist. A combination of smugness and disgust, no doubt. At least he was gentleman enough not to say anything out loud.

"Is there a reason you're calling?" she

asked. "Because otherwise, I would like to go back to dying."

"Actually, there are two reasons, if you can stave off your demise for ten minutes."

"I'll try, but I'm not making any promises. What do you need?"

"The first thing isn't a need, it's an invitation. Rosalind and I were talking last night. About how fantastical the last eighteen months have been. Between her accident and last Christmas…"

Fantastical was a good word for it. Eighteen months earlier, Rosalind had disappeared after her car plunged off a bridge in Scotland. She had reappeared last Christmas hundreds of miles away with amnesia of all things. Rediscovering their relationship had been a challenge. Susan liked to think she helped the cause by sharing some hard truths Thomas hadn't been willing to tell his returning bride.

Of course she was the only one who thought so at the time, but the three of them had put the issue behind them.

"We thought, with the baby arriving soon, it would be the perfect time to reestablish ourselves as a family," Thomas continued.

"What do you mean?"

"We've decided to renew our vows on

Christmas Eve. Nothing huge. Just family and a few close friends."

"That sounds…lovely." Susan hated the tiny knot of jealousy that twisted in her midsection. Her brother had fought hard for his life and family; a proper sister wouldn't envy his happiness.

Especially when his voice hummed with a bashful excitement. "Maddie's going to be the maid of honor," he said. "She'll be heartbroken if her favorite aunt isn't there."

"I'd be heartbroken if I missed seeing her," Susan replied, the knot easing slightly. The prospect of seeing her young niece dressed like a princess was too charming to resist.

"So you'll be there?"

"Of course." It wasn't like she had Christmas Eve plans.

"Great. I'll let Rosalind know. The other reason I called…" On the other end of the line, Susan heard the clink of a teacup. "I'm going to need you and Linus to host the Collier party again this year. I promised Rosalind I would take time off when the baby was born so we could bond as a family."

Susan groaned. Not again. Collier's had been holding a company Christmas party for its employees ever since the days of Queen

Victoria. What was once a show of largesse toward the workers had morphed into a fancy cocktail party hosted by the CEO. Last year, Thomas had begged off because of Rosalind's amnesia, leaving her and Linus to play the benevolent owners.

"Can't Linus host by himself?" Everyone loved Linus.

"I'd prefer both of you to be there. Especially since Linus has been…"

"Unreliable?" She thought of how he'd left her in the lurch last night.

"Distracted," Thomas replied. There was a pause, during which she imagined him studying his cup of tea while he thought of the right words. "Look, I know the party's not your favorite event…"

"Try least favorite," Susan corrected. The whole affair was an exercise in awkwardness for everyone involved. Smiling and making small talk with people like Ginger and Courtney. It'd be like the wedding times ten. "I was actually thinking of staying home this year…"

"You can't. You're a Collier. It wouldn't look right."

"I doubt people will care—they're more interested in the free booze."

"Susan…"

"Fine." She noticed he hadn't corrected her. "I'll host the party."

"Thank you."

"Is there anything else or can I go back to dying now?" Her head was demanding coffee and aspirin before it could handle any more conversation.

"Die away," her brother replied.

They said their goodbyes, and Susan tossed her phone on the cushion next to her. Five minutes, she thought as her eyes fluttered closed and her body fell sideways. Five minutes and she'd head to the kitchen for caffeine.

The phone rang again, the shrillness next to her ear making her wince. She fumbled for it without opening her eyes. "What did you forget?"

"Nothing that I know of," said an unfamiliar voice. Deep and with a strong northern twang, it caused tingles to trip up her spine. "I was calling to see how your head felt this morning."

How did this stranger know she had a killer hangover? "Who is this?" Susan pushed herself into a seated position—again.

"Lewis Matolo. The bloke who brought you home, remember?"

Remember? She was hoping to forget. Nearly bursting into tears, tripping over her own two feet. She'd worked hard her entire adult life to project an image of togetherness and control to the outside world…and Lewis Matolo had seen none of that.

She also remembered him being incredibly attractive. If you were into the cocky, athletic sort.

"How did you get my number?"

"I texted Hank and Maria and asked them."

"You bothered them on their honeymoon." Her heart actually fluttered at the idea. Why on earth would he go to that much trouble to track her down? Surely, not simply to check on her well-being.

"Don't worry. They were killing time at Heathrow waiting for their boarding call. I'm glad to see you made it to your apartment safely. No tripping up the stairs?"

Thankfully, he couldn't see how warm her face was. "I told you, the sidewalk was slippery from the cold weather," she said.

"Uh-huh." It was clear from the amusement in his voice that he hadn't bought the excuse then and he still wasn't buying it now. Susan blushed a little deeper.

"Since you didn't fall and break your

neck," he continued, "how would you feel about lunch?"

"Lunch? With you?" A dumb question, she knew, but he'd caught her off guard. She needed a reality check before her heart fluttered again. Why would someone like him be asking her out?

"No, with Prince William. I have a…business proposition to run by you."

How stupid of her. Of course he would be calling about business. Doing her best to hold back a sigh, she said, "New business ideas are my brother Thomas's bailiwick. You're better off calling him directly. I don't get involved in that end."

"You misunderstand. This isn't about Collier's. It's about… Let me just say I think I have an idea that might benefit us both."

Beneficial to her but didn't involve Collier's? He had her attention. "Go on?"

"I don't suppose you've read Lorianne's blog today?"

Lorianne Around London was the UK's most popular gossip website. A treasure trove of royal, political and celebrity gossip, the blog was influential and widely read, even by those who claimed they didn't. "The only thing I've seen today is the inside of my eye-lids. Why?"

"You might want to check it out on your way to the restaurant," Lewis replied. "There's a "Blind Item" you might find interesting. Now, are we on for lunch?"

Susan ran a hand through her curls. Her hair was a stiff mess from being retro-styled and she still had a splitting headache. Without checking a mirror, she knew she looked like a plump, raccoon-eyed nightmare. Hardly suitable for public viewing.

On the other hand, Lewis's offer intrigued her foggy brain. A business venture that benefitted her, didn't involve Collier's and was somehow connected to a "Blind Item" in *Lorianne Around London*? How could she resist?

"Where and when?" she asked.

The Christmas tree next to the fountain was decorated with pairs of miniature shoes. At night, it was lit with hundreds of rainbow-colored lights, but at midday all you could see were mini sneakers and stilettos. It was supposed to be making an artistic and social commentary, but damn if Lewis could figure it out. Walk a mile in another's shoes, maybe? Guess he wasn't sophisticated enough because he preferred the lights.

Still frowning, he turned his attention back to the restaurant. It was ten minutes past their agreed-upon time. Susan didn't strike him as the kind of person who ran late. He'd done a little digging on her when he'd texted Hank and Maria. If anything, Susan was the kind of person who arrived early and grew annoyed when you didn't too. She hadn't been joking last night when she said she wasn't very well liked at her company. In fact, Maria had used a very specific word to describe her, and for a second Lewis wondered if his plan was a good idea.

He caught the eye of a waiter who immediately approached the table. "Can I get another sparkling water?" he asked.

The young man nodded. "Of course. Right away."

As the man walked away, Lewis noticed a handful of diners looking in his direction. The Mayfair restaurant was too posh a location for autograph seekers. The people who dined here were supposed to be nonchalant about dining with celebrities. That didn't mean they weren't above sneaking a peek when one was in their midst, however.

When he was a kid, places like this were a foreign country. They were for people who lived on the other side of the city, who drove nice cars and whose kids always had new clothes. They definitely weren't for nobodies who bounced from foster home to foster home. Sometimes he pinched himself that he was really able to walk into a restaurant like this one and order whatever he wanted. Sometimes he masked his anxiety with extreme cockiness.

Sometimes—most times, in the past—he'd drunk to keep from feeling exposed.

It's all right; you belong here.

For how long though? Celebrity was a fleeting thing. Washed-up athletes were a dime a dozen. If he couldn't get a broadcast job, what would he do? Football was the only world he knew. The sport defined him. Made him matter. Made him *somebody.*

It's your reputation, Lewis. That's how his agent had put it after telling him he'd lost the BBC commentator job. *People are afraid you're going to pull one of your antics again. No one wants to risk waking up to see their studio analyst double-fisting bottles of Cristal on the front page.*

In other words, he needed to prove to the

world he had shed his Champagne Lewis persona for good. He'd been trying to deliver that message for the past nine months, but karma kept tripping him up. Like last night. He was surprised that the drink-tossing incident hadn't made it onto Lorianne's blog. The woman had spies everywhere.

Reading today's item, however, made him realize a few things. First, that he was damn lucky, and second, that if he wanted the world to know he was a changed man, he needed to do more than simply give up drinking and stay home. He needed to give the public proof, something splashy, that would convey the message for him.

The idea as to how had hit him like a jolt this morning. It was crazy, but it was worth a shot.

Now he needed his proposed partner in crime to appear.

He was about to turn his awareness back to the window when a flash of blue caught his attention. Finally. Susan Collier cut through the dining room, her peacock blue jacket popping amid the room's gold-and-green garlands. She wore a pair of oversize sunglasses covering her face and moved like a person who didn't have a moment to spare. Quite a different appearance from the soft, hazy woman who'd tripped her way up her front stairs the night before.

"Sorry I'm late. We got stuck in traffic."

Lewis saw it for the excuse it was. He also always seemed to have problems with the traffic on days he was hungover. "No problem. I've been sitting hear enjoying the view. It's beginning to look a lot like Christmas."

"It should. They started decorating the day after Halloween."

She looked down at the bench he sat on. Although the alcove table could accommodate up to six people, it had been set for intimacy. This meant the only seating was the velvet bench that curved along the wall. She had no choice but to slide to the middle so they could sit side by side. "Interesting choice of table," she remarked.

"I like sitting by the window." He moved over to make room. Not too much room though. He wanted to sit next to her. That was the point.

"Don't suppose you read Lorianne's site," he said when she'd settled in—her sunglasses remaining in place.

"You mean 'Blind Item' number five? How could I resist? You had me intrigued." Reaching into her shoulder bag, she pulled out a neatly folded piece of paper. It was a printout of Lorianne's blog.

This A-plus bad-boy former athlete with the fancy name was seen playing the gentleman for a member of one of London's most established families last night. He walked the lady to the door and didn't stay the night. Fluke? Or has he washed his hands of his wild ways?

She folded the paper in half again. "Those are some of the lamest clues I've ever seen. 'Fancy name' for Champagne Lewis? 'Washed his hands' for Collier's Soap? Was this your doing?"

"I wish. Our driver must have given her the tip. Lorianne's known for her network. He must have texted her after he dropped us off and Lorianne shoved it in her column." That was the beauty of the internet. In the old days, the public would have had to wait another twenty-four hours for the news item to go public.

"Interesting, don't you think?" he asked.

"How so?" Susan replied.

"Good afternoon. Glad you could join us."

It was their waiter, returning with Lewis's sparkling water. "Can I get you anything? A cocktail perhaps?"

"The lady will have a Bloody Mary." Lewis ignored the way Susan's head spun around to stare at him.

"A glass of water will be fine," she told the waiter, in a no-nonsense tone.

"And the Bloody Mary."

The poor young man looked from Lewis to Susan and back, clearly unsure who he should listen to. "She'll have water and a Bloody Mary," Lewis told him. He leaned in so he could lower his voice. "Hair of the dog, Trust me."

"And if I don't?"

"You'll be nursing that headache of yours all day." A drink wouldn't ease the pain of her throbbing head necessarily, but in his experience, it helped more often than not. "I'm the expert, remember?"

"Fine." She told the waiter to bring her both. "If alcohol is such a cure-all, why aren't you having any?" she asked once the waiter had gone.

"Simple. I'm not hungover. Plus, I don't drink. Anymore," he added when she opened her mouth.

"You don't? Since when?"

Since he'd woken up with one too many hangovers and realized what a mess he'd made of his career, that's when. "Been nearly nine months now."

"Oh. I didn't realize."

"Few people do." And those who did, didn't believe it would stick. "I decided last spring it was time to get my act together. Turn over a new leaf, as it were."

"How's the new leaf working out for you?"

"There's been a few bumps." Like last night. "Turns out being sober is only half the battle. Dealing with the mess you left behind..."

"I'm guessing last night was a bump."

"For both of us, wouldn't you say?" He took a sip of water. "Are you going to wear those glasses throughout lunch?" It was impossible to gauge her expression when it was hidden by those big black lenses. "Feel like I'm having lunch with a Russian spy." Or a woman embarrassed to be with him.

Although her lips pulled into a smirk, she removed the glasses. "Satisfied?" she asked.

Her excess from the night before revealed itself in a pair of dark circles that washed the color from her face. Her eyes' warm copper center was still visible though. Lewis had wondered if he'd imagined the unusual color. He hadn't. He hadn't imagined the intelligence in her eyes either.

"So…" She dropped her gaze, blocking his view once more. "You said you had a business proposition for me."

"Yes." Apparently they were going to get right down to business. Lewis could deal with that. "Now that I've retired, I'm hoping to get into broadcasting but no one wants to give me so much as a meeting. They're all afraid to take a risk."

"No offense, but can you blame them?"

"Maybe once upon a time, but I'm not the same guy I was nine months ago. I've grown up, and if they gave me a shot, they would see that I know my stuff. I'd be damned good."

He shifted in his seat so he could look her straight on. "It's maddening. They won't even meet with me. It's as though the world has slotted me into a role and now I'm stuck in it for life. Whether it fits or not."

"Everyone thinks they know you," she said in soft voice. She was folding and unfolding her glasses with great thoughtfulness.

"Precisely." The rush of someone understanding made Lewis want to grab her hands and squeeze them. "Telling them isn't enough. They need tangible evidence that I am not the same person. That's where you come in." Taking a chance, he reached over and laid his hand on her forearm.

In a flash, her hands stilled. Lewis felt the muscles in her arm tense. Slowly—very slowly—her gaze rose to meet his. "How so?"

Before he could answer, their waiter returned. As the man placed her drinks on the table, his eyes flickered to Susan's arm, which she quickly pulled away. Lewis tried not to smile. "Are you ready to order?" the waiter asked.

So eager had he been to discuss business, neither of them had had a chance to look at the menu. "Not—"

"I'll have the egg-and-avocado sandwich," Susan announced. "Is that all right? Or do you need to change my order?"

Man, but she had a bite to her. And here he'd thought last night's sharpness was from the alcohol. "Sounds perfect. In fact, I'll have the same. You're very decisive, for a woman who didn't have time to study the menu," he said once the waiter had moved on."

"I read the item at the top of the page and decided it sounded good. I'm not much for hemming and hawing when there's a decision to be made."

"You don't like to waste your time."

"Not if I can help it." She swished her celery-stalk garnish around in the glass and took a crisp bite off its end. "Bringing me back to my question. What are you looking for from me?"

Lewis placed his hands on the table. He thought about covering her arm again, but that might look too forward. This was where actions and word choice mattered. "You might think I'm crazy, but I got the idea from Lorianne's site. Until now, I've been staying out of the public eye, hoping people would realize I'd given up the party life, but it hasn't been working. People only believe what they see."

"Or think they see," she added.

She caught on quick. "Precisely. This morning, I read Lorianne's 'Blind Item,' and I realized I had things backward. Instead of being out of the public eye, I need to do the opposite. I need to be seen as much as possible, only, in the way I *want* to be seen."

"In other words, you want to create a new tabloid persona. Makes sense. Although I'm not sure where I come in."

"Well…" This was where the proposition got tricky. "I was hoping you'd be my partner in crime," he said. "Nothing says *changed man* like a relationship with someone completely against type. A woman who is the total opposite of all the other women I've ever dated. You."

Susan stared at him, drink hovering just below her lower lip. "Are you trying to get another drink tossed in your face?"

"Wait." She'd set her drink down and was gathering her things. "Hear me out."

"I already heard you. You spent your sporting career dating beautiful women. Now, to prove you've changed, you want to date someone who isn't beautiful and that someone is me."

"That's not what I meant at all."

"Really?" She cocked her head. "What did I miss?"

"Yes, I dated a lot of beautiful women, but…" He threw up his hands in case the noise she'd made was the precursor to a drink toss. "They were just good-time girls."

"The kind of girls whose name you forget."

"Right. I mean, no. You should never, ever forget a lover's name." He could almost hear the thin ice cracking beneath him with each sentence. So much for making sure his words mattered.

"You're smart," he rushed on. "You own a respected business. Doesn't Collier's Soap have the queen's blessing?"

"We have a Royal Warrant, yes."

"See? You're someone society takes seriously. No one would expect to see you involved with a party boy like me. So if you *were* involved..."

"They would assume you must not be the empty-headed wild man anymore."

Forgetting about overstepping, he clasped her hand in his. "That's it exactly."

Her fingers were cold and damp from her glass. Lewis pressed his hands tight to warm them. "And it's not as though you're unattractive," he added.

She didn't smile. So much for humor. He was mucking this up big-time. "Look, you're smart. You're cute." Cute wasn't the right word, he realized. She radiated too much class and intelligence to be labeled merely cute. Sophisticated? Maybe. Different?

Yeah, different. Unique.

"Bottom line is, I need your help, if I'm to have any chance of getting a network job," he said. "Lorianne has already marked us as a potential couple. It would take a while to find another woman as qualified." Not to mention one whose company he enjoyed as much as he did Susan's, surprisingly.

"Why is being a broadcaster so important?" she asked. "Surely there are other jobs out there?"

"Because I think I'd be good at it. No, I know I'd be good at it," he told her. There was more though. "Besides, football is the only thing I've ever known. I'm not ready to leave it behind."

The field and the fans had been the only real home he'd ever had. Without them, all he'd have would be a handful of hazy memories of the glory days. He wasn't ready to be kicked to the curb, unwanted, again. To go back to being nobody.

He blinked. Susan was frowning at him from over her drink.

"Were you even listening?" she asked.

"Sorry. I drifted off for a moment."

"Obviously." She took a long sip of her drink, which, Lewis noticed, was about a third gone. "You said on the phone this proposition would be mutually beneficial. You explained what you would get out of this 'arrangement,' but what's in it for me?"

"Simple," he replied. "You get seen with me."

* * *

Thank goodness she'd swallowed before he spoke or she would have spit tomato juice all over the table. "You're joking. That's your idea of mutually beneficial?"

He leaned back against the bench, his arms stretched out along the back. "You disagree?"

Talk about ego. Like he was such a prize.

She took in his chiseled features—far more prominent in the light of day—and the way his cashmere sweater pulled across his equally chiseled torso.

Okay, he *was* a prize.

Still, did he think her so desperate she needed a fake boyfriend?

Aren't you? She ignored her own question.

"I think you have an extremely high opinion of your appeal." She paused to sip her drink. Much as she hated to admit it, the combination of tomato juice and vodka was easing her hangover. The tension in her shoulders and neck were lessening with each sip. "Why would I care whether I was seen in public with you?"

"To quote… 'my own brother didn't want to be my date.'"

"When did I say that?" It was true, but she couldn't see herself sharing the information.

"While we were waiting for the car."

Susan thought back. Much of the trip home was fuzzy. She vaguely remembered growing angry when they passed the ladies' room and going on a tirade about being single which may have morphed into a drunken pity party.

Oh, man, now she remembered. Stupid Christmas Wishes. "I was drunk. People say and do a lot of foolish things when they are under the influence, as I'm sure you would agree."

"In vino veritas."

He flashed a smirk as he reached for his water. "As for the value of my appeal...? There are a lot of women in the UK who would tell you I've got plenty."

"Then why don't you ask one of them to be your fake girlfriend? Oh, wait, let me guess. Oh, right, they're all supermodels and party girls."

"You're not going to let that go, are you? I was trying to lighten the mood."

"Doesn't change the fact that you clearly need me more than I need you." Or the way it stung.

"You're right," he replied. "I do need you more than you need me."

Points for honesty. Sitting back, she waited to hear his expanded sales pitch.

"Believe it or not, you would get something tangible out of the relationship," he told her.

Beyond being able to rub the fake arrangement in Ginger's and Courtney's faces—which she had to admit, a part of her found appealing. "How so?"

"If my plan works, the two of us will be in the tabloids and gossip columns, a lot. Both our profiles will be raised."

"Why would I care about a higher profile?"

"You tell me, Ms. Collier."

He was appealing to her ego again. It wouldn't be only the Courtneys and Gingers of the world she'd be showing, it would be the world. The equivalent of a giant ad announcing her desirability. As if she were that lonely.

"What makes you think the tabloids, or anyone for that matter, would believe we were a real couple?" she asked. Simply out of curiosity.

"Are you kidding? Celebrities arrange public relationships all the time in order to sell an image. Remember that pop star who was dating the guy from the Brazilian team? Totally to keep people from knowing he was shagging his equipment manager."

"No way."

"It's the truth. I know the equipment manager."

Susan remembered seeing the singer on the cover of several magazines at the hair salon talking about finally finding love. She'd been a nobody newcomer before the relationship.

A thought suddenly occurred to her. "You're not…?"

"No."

Not that it mattered. She still wasn't going to say yes to this silly idea.

"Granted you and I wouldn't become an international sensation, but, if we do this right, we will get mentioned in the papers. We only need to be together a few months. Long enough for people to believe we are the real deal."

"Even though we aren't."

"Right. But the only people who will know are you and me. Everyone else will think you won me over with your brilliant mind and razor-sharp wit."

"And, if I say yes—not that I am—how long would we need to play act?"

"Just over a month. At least through the holidays."

Meaning he would be her "boyfriend" at the Collier's Christmas Party. Wouldn't that be interesting? To be part of a couple for once instead of standing around watching everyone else? Even if it was only pretend.

Despite his offered upsides, the idea struck her wrong. Did she really want to spend weeks with a disinterested man just so she could stick it to a few petty witches? Seemed like she should be better than that.

Then there was the obvious.

"Wouldn't it be easier to simply date a different category of women instead of subterfuge?"

He looked at her for a second, as though weighing his words, his sensual lips drawn in a frown. "If I were looking to get into a long-term relationship, maybe, but…"

"You don't have to go on. I get your point." He was looking to repair an image, not actually change his tastes.

"I'm not asking you to decide this very moment," he said. "Let's have some lunch, and you think the idea over. Let me know later on."

"Thank you." She doubted food would

change her mind, but she'd rather not ruin the mood until after she'd eaten.

In the meantime, she was curious if she still looked like death now that her headache had eased. When the waiter arrived with their food, she excused herself and went to the ladies' room.

Whoever decorated the restaurant had the foresight to install ambient lighting as opposed to fluorescent in the sitting room so women checking the mirror would feel good about their appearance. Unfortunately, all the ambient lighting in the world couldn't brighten her washed-out complexion. She'd tried to hide the damage with powder and concealer, but the dark circles stubbornly remained. Searching into her bag, she pulled out a compact and touched up her blush. No sense bothering with lipstick since it would only wear off again when she ate. Then she combed her hands through her curls and stepped back.

Her shoulders slumped. She looked like she felt. Tired, and hungover. The jacket was too boxy for her short frame, making her look like a squashed blueberry. People probably thought she was Lewis's agent or business manager. Certainly not a potential girlfriend. Correction, fake girlfriend.

What made Lewis think the idea would work? No way, people wouldn't believe they were an item.

Behind her, the door opened and two university-age girls slipped in. Susan immediately envied their long hair which they wore in messy topknots. Envied their cropped sweaters and leggings too. No one would mistake them for a sports agent.

All her life, she had wondered what it would be like to *fit*. To feel accepted by someone. Anyone. She had a lot to offer, if people would only look.

Don't be so dramatic, her mother would say. *People don't look if there's nothing to look at.*

Belinda was full of those little bon mots.

Lewis Matolo was offering people something to look at.

Would it be so horrible if the world saw her as someone different? Just for a little while?

Rummaging through her bag, she located a hair tie and forced her curls into a messy bun. Then, she shed her jacket. The black turtleneck wasn't stylish, but at least the world could see she had a waist.

The world. Susan chewed her lower lip. Was she really that crazy?

Lewis was biting into his egg sandwich when she returned. She tossed her bag on the bench and slid in next to him. "You've got a deal."

CHAPTER THREE

"ARE YOU SURE?"

"Positive," Susan replied. "You don't have to keep asking."

But Lewis felt like he did. They were on their second cup of tea. An entire meal had gone by and he was having trouble processing the fact that she'd agreed to play his girlfriend. "I'm surprised, is all," he said. Flummoxed was a better word. "You didn't look very enthusiastic when I pitched the idea." Which was why, when she'd come back from the washroom and announced she was all in, he'd been floored.

"I'll admit, the plan sounds insane, but it's only for a short time, right? Not like you're proposing marriage or anything."

"Dating only, I promise." Marriage was one of those concepts that made his insides squeeze, along with commitment and emotions. As it was, this arrangement would be the longest relationship he'd ever had. Then again, so would anything longer than a three-day weekend.

Her smile seemed to tighten for a second. "Right," she said, setting her teacup down. "How does this work? Do we draw up contracts? Write out conditions? What does one do in a fake relationship?"

Fortunately, Lewis had given the matter some thought on the off chance she'd agree. "Obviously, the goal is to be seen together in as many different settings as possible. Like a real couple."

"And we do this until the tabloids notice?" she asked while pouring the last of her tea. "I know you're considered a tabloid magnet, but that doesn't seem terribly efficient."

"You're right, it's not. That's why I'm going to have my agent leak a few discreet comments. We're also going to have to attend one or two social events where there's press. Actually, I've drawn up a few notes laying out how I think this plan should proceed."

He reached into his back pocket and pulled out a folded piece of paper. Moving his teacup aside, he smoothed it flat. "We want everyone to see us, but at the same time we want to look subtle—like this is the real deal—so I've come up with a progression of steps."

Susan's arm pressed against his as she leaned in to get a better view. "Date at a public venue. Attend a society event. Be seen doing coupley Christmas things?" She turned to look at him. "Coupley Christmas things?"

"You know, Christmas shopping or walking in Kew Gardens. Whatever it is women drag their boyfriends to do during the holidays."

"I see. Clearly, you've given this a lot of thought."

"Did you think I would invite you to lunch without some kind of plan in mind?" Lewis replied. He wasn't stupid. If Susan had said yes, he knew a woman like her would expect details. "You're going to have to start giving me a little more credit."

Then again, could he blame her? The whole point behind this charade was to prove he had more to offer than being a drunken party boy.

"Considering I didn't know fake girlfriends really existed until ninety minutes ago, you'll have to cut me some slack. I do have one question," she said, tapping her cup. "How can we be sure people—the tabloids—will believe us?"

It was a reasonable question. The honest answer was they couldn't. Not entirely. "I get the impression that as long as the story gets attention, they—the papers—won't dig too deep," he told her. "However, you bring up a point I hadn't thought about. Lorianne has spies everywhere—it's how she gets her scoops—so we'll need to make sure we act like a couple whenever we're together, even when we think no one's paying attention."

"Is that why we're having lunch in a cozy corner booth? Again, I'm impressed."

Lewis was flattered. It wasn't often that the woman he was with complimented his intelligence. Other skills usually took priority. "Thank you," he said. "Oh, and another thing…we need to keep this arrangement between us. No one but you, me and my agent, Michael, will know. Will that be a problem?"

She shook her head. "I'd already assumed the arrangement would be need-to-know. If it were a problem, I wouldn't have agreed in the first place."

Good. They were on the same page.

"What are you doing?"

She'd taken a pen out of her bag and was making notes on the paper. Lewis watched her write the words *Christmas Party* with a date. "My brother Thomas has informed me that I'm cohosting the corporate Christmas party again this year. I think it's only fair that my 'boyfriend' attend with me."

"Corporate Christmas party, huh?"

"For employees and other people we do business with. The ad agency, banks, etc."

He had to admit he'd wondered if she'd insist on some type of work-related couple appearance after her speech last night. "This wouldn't be to show up those ladies from the bathroom, would it?"

Her shrug was enough of an answer.

Whatever. It was fine with him if she wanted to put a few people in their place. "I'll mark my calendar. While we're scheduling, do you need me to play arm candy for any other events? New Year's Eve? Christmas Day?"

"As it so happens…" She suddenly stopped and shook her head. "Never mind. The Christmas party will be enough."

"Are you sure?" She was holding back.

"Yes, I'm sure. Now please stop asking that question." Clicking her pen, she wrote the word *Agreed* at the top of the page along with her name and the date. When finished, she held out the pen. "Since you didn't answer my question about a contract, I hope this will do."

"Seeing as how I would have settled for a handshake...?" He added his signature below hers. It was official: one image makeover in a half dozen assorted steps. Whether it would work was anyone's guess.

"I now pronounce us a couple," he announced.

For better or for worse.

What had she gotten herself into? "When you said we were going to watch a basketball game, I thought you meant at a pub," Susan said. Some quaint place with brick walls and a fireplace. "Not surrounded by twenty thousand spectators at London's O2 arena."

She was decidedly overdressed in a pencil skirt and heels. For some insane reason she'd decided to dress daringly. Her way of showing the world she was worthy of Lewis's attention. Now she felt stupid.

"I didn't know London even had a basketball team," she said as they walked up the ramp.

"There's an entire league," Lewis answered, "but they don't play here. This is a special event. Two American teams."

That explained the crowds. It didn't explain why he'd chosen a basketball game for their first date though, so she asked.

"Why else? To send a message. I wanted people to see that I'm more than a footballer. I appreciate all sports."

"Thus broadening your appeal as a broadcaster. Clever."

"Thank you."

They stepped out of the ramp into the brightly lit arena filled with people. Susan had been to the O2 before, for concerts, but this was the first time she'd seen it prepped for a sports event. Below them, American basketball players were warming up on the shiny parquet floor. "Our seats are down there," Lewis said in her ear as he pointed toward the court. His hand molded to the small of her back as he guided her down the steep steps.

They were really doing this. Pretending they were a couple. Her legs began to shake and from more than just navigating the steep stairs in stilettos. She gripped the railing.

"What's wrong?"

She didn't realize she'd stopped moving until Lewis spoke. He looked at her, his brown eyes narrowed in concern. "Sorry.

I— It just dawned on me that we're on a date."

"You're only figuring that out now?"

"You know what I mean."

"Not really," he replied.

Until this moment, their arrangement had been conceptual. She hadn't thought about the fact that in order to be taken for a real couple, they would have to behave like a real couple. Which made this evening a date complete with all the touching and other date-like behavior. Lewis was going to have to pretend he was attracted to her. Did he really think they could pull this off?

They were blocking the stairs. That was one way to attract attention. "Never mind," she said. "It doesn't matter."

"If you say so."

Their seats were in the middle of the row, close to the front, but high enough they could see the entire court. They also had a clear view of the giant electronic screen that hung over center court. It was like having a one-hundred-inch television in your living room.

She looked around at the people milling about. "I doubt anyone will notice us in this crowd," she commented.

"Oh, they'll notice us," Lewis replied. He

leaned closer, his nose practically nuzzling the outer shell of her ear. "My agent has arranged for us to be outed after the third quarter."

Outed? This time she had to lean into him. "What do you mean?"

"You'll see," he replied with a grin. "Just keep your eye on the scoreboard."

She stared at the screen, which at the moment was playing an advertisement for a Christmas concert. "I don't like surprises," she told him.

"You're going to have to get used to them if you're planning to hang around with me."

Why? Was he that spontaneous?

Check that. They were talking about a man who had once jumped naked off a boat into the Thames.

Susan looked at the man folded into the seat beside her. His eyes were shining as he watched the action below. He looked back and forth, taking in everything that was going on. "You're not going to do something outrageous are you?" she asked.

"Yeah. I've got the words *I love Susan Collier* painted on my chest. I'm planning to tear off me shirt so everyone can read them."

She rolled her eyes. "Very funny."

"You're the one who asked the silly question." Before she could respond, he reached over and patted her knee, his large hand warm and firm in its touch. "Relax. This is about changing my image, remember? Plus, I'm sober," he added. "I'm far less outrageous without the alcohol."

Ironic, then, that they should meet because of her drunkenness.

"What made you stop drinking?"

It was a question she had wanted to ask. He looked so at peace with the decision, she was curious. She wasn't surprised when he shrugged as though the decision was no big deal. "Forgot one too many names. Jumped into one too many fountains."

"I would think one fountain would be too many." She gasped when he held up three fingers. "You're kidding."

"We can go for four if you're feeling adventurous. Seriously though," he said, the smile leaving his eyes, "when my career ended, so did the party. When you're on top of the world, being a wild man makes you cool. When you're out of the spotlight, you're just a washed-up drunk. I decided I'd rather try to climb back to the top and maybe remember it this time."

As offhand as he tried to sound, there was no mistaking the regret in his voice. Susan took a good look at the man to whom she'd bound herself for the upcoming weeks. If you looked past the chiseled features, you could see the signs of a life lived hard. She spied tiny scars on his chin and cheekbones and the bump of a broken nose.

"Do you miss playing?" she asked.

"Only every bloomin' day." He pointed to the court where the American players were shooting basketballs at the basket. "See that player there? Number twenty-three? He's the best basketball player in the world."

"Okay." He looked like all the other players to Susan.

"Everyone in this building is here to see him," Lewis told her. "Sure, they care about the other players too, but him…he's the reason they came."

"Because he's the best."

"Exactly. I can't begin to describe what it's like. Being on the pitch, knowing everyone is pinning their game hopes on you and your ability. Feeling the love of thousands. There's no high like it. And when you're in the middle of playing, it's like there's nothing else in the world. There's you, and the ball and the match."

His faraway gaze was so beautiful, it made Susan's throat catch.

"You were really good, weren't you?" she said, embarrassed that she didn't know.

"I was the best. When I was at the top of my game, no one could beat me." She believed him. The arrogance had too much certainty behind it to be false.

"How did you start playing?" She turned in her seat so she could look at him while he spoke. The expressions on his profile were far more interesting than anything going on below.

"Just started," he said with a shrug. "Neighborhood kids played in the street—I asked if I could play. No one else wanted to tend goal, so they let me."

"Let me guess. Soon as they saw you play they made you permanent."

A grin slid across his face. "Pretty much. After that, I played for whatever team I could until I was signed by Manchester for their academy team."

"Your parents must have been proud." Remembering the way her father used to beam every time Thomas or Linus achieved one of their many achievements, she could only imagine how his family had felt when their son joined the Premier League Under 16 program.

"Doubt they knew. I lived with foster families until I was old enough to live in digs at the academy. Never met my dad, and Mum couldn't get off the drugs. The smack pulled her back every time."

Dear Lord.

"I'm sorry."

"Don't be. I don't even remember the woman at this point. She's more of a blur than anything. What about your parents?"

"My dad died a few years ago and my mother…" Her mother wasn't a topic the family liked to talk about. "My mom is an actress. Belinda Quinn."

"That name sounds familiar."

"She played the sexy neighbor on *The Confidents*."

"Was that the show where some poor guy inherited a ton of money from somebody and they moved to a swanky neighborhood?" His bare-bones description was about as deep as the show. "I used to watch old episodes when I was a kid. Your mom was a looker."

"She was *something*," Susan replied. "Except into being a mother. My dad's fault she got saddled with an albatross of a daughter."

"She didn't actually say that, did she?"

Susan put on a haughty voice. "Damn near ruined her figure, I did, and her career. Not to mention the whole messy business of kids demanding attention all the time. After all, what about *her* needs?" She picked at the lint on her sweater. "My mother has what they call histrionic, narcissistic personality disorder. A fancy way of saying she's a self-centered lunatic," she said when he frowned. "Psychology's a bit of a hobby for me. I've done a lot of reading." A desperate attempt to understand why her mother didn't want her. "Anyway, when she and my father divorced, she relinquished custody. We've shared maybe a dozen words since."

"How old were you when she left?" Lewis asked.

"Eight. I came home from school and she'd gone. Last words she said to me were 'Not now, Susan, I've got a headache.'"

"So both our mothers took a flyer. Lucky us, we have something in common." Their eyes met and a beat of understanding passed between them.

Lewis cleared his throat. "Enough childhood talk. We're here to enjoy a basketball game, right?" With that, he began explaining the action on the court.

The evening passed quickly. Watching the game, with its fast pace and athleticism, was a lot more fun than Susan expected. For someone who claimed to know only a little about the game, Lewis had a very keen grip on the strategy. She imagined he would sound marvelous explaining football too. No wonder he wanted to be a commentator.

By the third quarter, they were both on their feet cheering for three-point shots.

"Exciting, isn't it?" Lewis remarked after two players came crashing together under the basketball net. "Gets the blood pumping." He popped a piece of her popcorn into his mouth with a grin. "Clock ticking. Everyone rushing at the same fast pace in organized chaos. It's fantastic."

Susan took in the glow on his face. The first two times they met, he'd been clean-shaven. Tonight, a five-o'clock shadow covered his cheeks, turning his classic-looking features dark and dangerous. Add the adrenaline shining in his eyes and the result was breathtaking. He was clearly in his element.

"You'd be amazing on television," she told him.

Her slip earned her a blush, enhancing what was already camera perfect. "Thanks," he said. "Nice to know someone thinks so. If only the networks were as enthusiastic."

If there was anything "*Shrewsan*" understood, it was being publicly judged without cause. Everyone was so certain they knew how she ticked. Without giving it a second thought, she squeezed his fingers. "We'll just have to do our best to make sure you get a shot."

On the floor, a buzzer rang announcing the end of the third quarter. While the players gathered around their respective benches, she and Lewis settled back into their seats. "I thought you said something was supposed to happen during the last quarter," she said. "Your agent didn't forget, did he?"

"Michael? No way. He's got a publicist on staff who knows her stuff. Bailed me out of public embarrassment more than once, she has."

"If something's going to happen, it's going to have to happen soon. According to the clock, there's only twelve minutes left in the game." She pointed to the center screen which was playing a highlight from a few minutes earlier.

When the highlight ended, an electronic Santa Claus came bouncing across the screen. He stopped, pointed upward and the words Mistletoe Camera scrolled by. The image fizzled away and suddenly, there was a view of the crowd. People cheered and waved as the camera zoomed in tighter and tighter until it focused on an unsuspecting couple. The pair laughed and shared a kiss.

"Mistletoe Camera?" She'd never heard of such an idea.

"An American thing," Lewis told her. "Big hit over there from what I hear. The promoters thought the gimmick might be fun to do here, as well. Crowd seems to be enjoying it."

The camera moved on, this time to a pair of middle-aged men who were clearly not together. Oblivious, they faced away from one another until the cheering crowd forced them to look up. As soon as they realized, they too broke out in laughter. The camera remained on them until they shared a bro hug.

"So it appears," she remarked. "Nothing says romance like thousands of people watching you kiss. Wait a second…?" How did Lewis know what the promoters had planned?

Her question was cut off by the crowd suddenly roaring louder than ever. She looked up at the screen to see why and her stomach dropped.

The Mistletoe Cam was pointed at *them*.

CHAPTER FOUR

"You…" THERE WAS a smile on her face, but Lewis could see the muscles twitching in her jaw. She was gritting her teeth.

"Wasn't me, luv. It was my agent." He murmured the words in her ear so that on camera it looked like they were sharing a secret.

While he was speaking, he slipped an arm around her shoulder. He knew as soon as Michael mentioned the promotion that Susan would hate the idea, which was why he'd kept the plans a secret. He didn't want to risk her looking annoyed for three periods. Or worse, walking out on him.

"You said yourself, nothing says you're in a relationship like kissing in front of ten thousand people."

"I was being sarcastic. I didn't mean we should follow suit."

"Why not? You've got to admit, it's a great

idea. At least the crowd thinks so." The egging on had gotten louder when he put his arm around her. Lewis leaned in closer. They had a limited window before the camera moved to another couple. "They're getting restless. Better give them what they want."

Her eyes widened. "You…you don't mind?"

Why would he mind? It was just a kiss. And she was an attractive woman. He'd been watching her smile and laugh all night long. When she relaxed, her softness came out. There was real vulnerability beneath the armor. The kind that made you want to treat her special. She really was adorable and begging to be cuddled.

"I'm game if you are," he replied. "What do you say? Ready to tell the world we're together?"

"Um…" She licked her lips, making them shiny and enticing. "Okay."

Good answer since he planned on kissing her anyway. Cupping her cheek with his free hand, he bent in for what he meant to be a gentle kiss. The crowd responded with applause. Emboldened by their enthusiasm, he let the kiss linger. Susan tasted delicious. Salt, artificial butter and something indefinable that had him tempted to lick his way past her lips.

When he finally did end the kiss, she looked up at him with what he swore was wonder in her darkened eyes. The look caused something primal to click deep inside him, and for a crazy second he thought about finding some dark corner where he could demonstrate how he really kissed a woman.

If they were in a real relationship, he would. In a heartbeat.

But they weren't. The kiss was simply a hook to sell a story, and what he thought was wonder in her eyes was probably nothing more than the arena lights reflecting in their greenness.

"What do you think?" he asked, leaning back in his seat. He'd keep his arm around her shoulders for now. "Believable?"

For the rest of the game, Susan tried her best not to look as stunned as she felt. If that was Lewis's idea of a casual first kiss, what did he do when he gave his full effort? It was all she could do not to crawl into his lap and beg for more.

She *should* be angry that he kept the plan

a secret. If she had known his plan involved the two of them putting on a public display, she would have...

What? Refused? Then she would have missed out on the most amazing kiss of her life. God bless the Mistletoe Cam, she decided. Were kisses like this what she could expect over the next few weeks? Well then, Merry Christmas to her.

Over her lifetime, Susan had grown accustomed to walking in on whispered conversations. It started at age five when her mother would end telephone conversations abruptly upon Susan entering the room. At the office, she could count on finding at least one or two employees with their heads together, usually complaining or gossiping. Whenever they saw her, they would break up and pretend they had been talking about work.

Today there seemed to be more heads together than usual, starting with a small group by the reception desk. Every single one of them had turned to look at her when she stepped through the front door. That could only mean one thing: There was a mention of last night in the paper.

Last night. She fought a smile as she

walked toward her office. Fake or not, she had had a terrific time.

When she concentrated, she could still feel Lewis's kiss. Of course, later that night he'd dropped her off at her apartment with nothing but a friendly hug, but she wouldn't dwell on that.

Upon reaching her office, she found Linus sitting on the edge of her desk. It was an annoying habit he had, that of refusing to use a chair. When he saw her, he pointed at her with a rolled-up newspaper. "If it isn't my sister, the cover girl."

"What are you getting on about? And get off my desk. You're messing up my piles." She hung her wool coat on the back of her door before shooing him off her work with a wave of her hand.

"I gather you haven't seen this morning's edition of the *Looking Glass*." He unfurled the newspaper. "I lied about the cover. Turns out you're more page-five material."

Grabbing the tabloid from Linus, she quickly flipped to the page. There, under the headline Merry Kiss-Mas was a photo of her and Lewis.

Wildman Champagne Lewis Matolo Looks

Tamed As He Cozies With A Mystery Lady, read the subhead.

The corners of her mouth twitched upward. The photographer had caught the moment just before they kissed. Her face was lifted to his, and they were looking at one another as if each were the only person in the room. There was a second photo too, which, from their excited expressions, looked like it was taken in the fourth quarter when they were cheering for a last-minute rally.

This explained all the odd looks. She gave in and let her smile bloom. Lewis had to be thrilled.

"You little minx. Why didn't you tell us you were seeing someone?"

She cast her brother a look over the top of the paper. "Minx? Seriously?"

"First word that came to mind, and you didn't answer my question. When did you start dating Lewis Matolo?"

"We..." Linus's question reminded her they hadn't worked out a proper backstory. Since she was alone, she was going to have to go with the obvious and fill Lewis in later. "We met at Maria's wedding. He went to school with her new husband. We shared a couple drinks in the bar and hit it off."

"A couple? Thomas said you were hung over when he spoke to you the next morning."

"Thomas has a big mouth, and what business is it of yours anyway?" Tucking the paper under her arm, she cast him another look as she made her way to her chair.

Much to her consternation, Linus followed, and perched himself on the edge of the desk again. "Is this where I say none?"

"Unless you'd like me to say it for you." Folding her arms, she sat back and waited for him to get to the point. Because there was a point; Linus always had a point. She just wished he'd hurry up because she wanted to call Lewis.

"Here's the thing," he said finally. "Normally, I'd agree with you, but in this case..."

"What do you mean, in this case?"

"Do you know who Lewis Matolo is? I mean really know?"

Of course she knew, and she knew exactly what Linus was driving at, as well. "Get to your point." Might as well hear him say it out loud.

Her brother tapped a knuckle against his lip, a habit he had when thinking. "How do I put this..."

"He's a drunken arse." Thomas Collier's

pronouncement entered the office two seconds before he did. The chairman of Collier's Soap strode into her office wearing his standard severe black suit. Dark and handsome, he was night to Linus's day.

Add Lewis to the mix and you would have one heck of a gorgeous trio, thought Susan. With her as the plump wrong note.

"Why don't you say it a little louder, Thomas? There might be a few people at the reception desk who didn't hear you," she snapped. "And he's not a drunken anything. Anymore. He stopped drinking."

"You just said you shared a couple drinks at the wedding," Linus said.

Oh, brother. She didn't realize they were going to analyze every single word. "*I* drank. *He* had water," she replied. "Not that what I do is any of your concern. In case you didn't notice, I'm a grown woman. I'm not required to explain my actions to you."

"Unless your actions blow back and bite Collier's," Thomas replied. "Do you have any idea the kinds of stunts this guy has pulled? Bar fights, drunken howlers."

"Stop it. I've read the headlines, same as you."

"Then you know he's a degenerate. Even

his teammates got tired of his antics. He bounced around to every team in the league because the other players hated dealing with him."

"Again, he *was* a degenerate. All of that happened when he was drinking." The ferocity of her defense surprised her, but she didn't like Thomas's tone. Her brothers didn't know Lewis. They didn't see the vulnerability in his eyes when he talked about his childhood. "There's a lot more to him than the headlines would lead you to believe." Her eyes glanced down at the newspaper and their photograph. "A lot more.

"Besides," she added, "I would think you'd be glad for the potential publicity. It is the Christmas season after all."

"Oh, sure," Thomas replied, "I'm thrilled to death. Nothing says Merry Christmas like having the company name tied to scandal."

"Oh, for crying out loud. There isn't going to be a scandal." Her big brother could be such a stubborn jerk. Once he got a notion in his head, he wouldn't shake it. "I would think you of all people would be open to the idea that people change."

That shut him up. They wouldn't be having a Christmas Eve vow renewal if Thomas and his wife hadn't learned to change. "Or do you think you and Rosalind have the monopoly on personal growth?"

"Don't be ridiculous. Of course, we don't," Thomas replied. "But…"

She finished the sentence for him. "Are you saying your relationship problems wouldn't have made headlines?"

"No, they would not have because neither of us was headline fodder." Implying that her "boyfriend" was and therefore their relationship would be in the press. It was all she could do not to tell him that was the point. In fact, if things went according to plan, the two of them would be all over the paper.

Her brother looked at her with the cool intensity he usually reserved for business meetings. "Two years," he said. "Two years, it took for me to get this company stable again after Dad ran it into the ground. Doing so very nearly cost me my marriage. The last thing I want is for it to be dragged down now by a scandal."

"For the last time, there won't be a scandal." The only way that could happen was if news of their fake relationship leaked out, and she and Lewis weren't planning to talk.

"We just want you to keep your wits about

you." As he so often did, Linus moved in as the voice of reason and distraction. "Guys like Lewis Matolo know how to play women to get what they want."

"You don't know anything," she told him. "You've never even met Lewis." And, so what if he was using her? Lewis had never been anything but honest regarding his intentions.

"I don't have to. Trust me, I know. We're cut from a similar cloth."

No, they weren't. The defense sprang to her lips despite her having zero evidence beyond a couple conversations, one of which centered around him using her to get what he wanted.

Linus leaned forward so his face was level with hers. "Look," he said. "We're not trying to be jerks here. We're simply looking out for our baby sister. We just don't want to see you get involved with something that might come back to haunt you."

Because God forbid her relationship have some kind of future.

That, she realized, was what really hurt. Not Thomas's worries about gossip, but their automatic assumption that her relationship was doomed. Was it so unbelievable to them that a man like Lewis could be attracted to her?

Granted it was a business arrangement but her brothers didn't know that. You'd think they would have a higher opinion of her choices.

But then why should they venture off script, right?

"I don't really care what you want," she snapped. Or what they thought of her either. "It's my life and who I date is my business. Now, if you don't mind, it's the end of the month. I have a whole bunch of work to do and you're sitting on my reports." Plus she needed to call Lewis so they could discuss their next step.

"Do what you want," Thomas said as Linus rose to his feet. "But you better be right about his being a different person. First negative article I see with the name Collier attached and I'll have your boyfriend's head on a platter." The toughness would have worked better if Linus hadn't snorted.

"He means his legal team will," her middle brother said. "Still, be careful, okay? Players are called players for a reason."

"Are we done with the lecture?" Susan asked. She really wanted to talk with Lewis now. Hoping they'd take the hint, she reached for her desk phone. It worked. They shut the door and left her in peace. Although Thomas did manage one last stern look through the glass wall.

Susan immediately picked up the paper to study the pictures again. Just who did they think they were, poking their noses in her love life? And Thomas calling Lewis a degenerate. Wait until the Collier's Christmas Party. She and Lewis would show everyone exactly how wrong their opinion was.

Even if they had to pretend to do so.

Has Champagne Lewis given up his wild ways? The former goaltender was seen canoodling with a brunette mystery woman at the O2 arena last night.

Sources say this isn't the first time the couple has been seen together. The two were spotted at Esprit last weekend enjoying a romantic Sunday brunch.

Lewis slapped the tabloid on the table with a grin. "Not bad," he said. "Not bad at all." There were two things the press loved: a good celebrity romance and a good redemption story. He should have thought of this plan months ago.

His eyes dropped to the photograph of him

and Susan. Thankfully she wasn't too annoyed about the "Mistletoe Cam" incident. Yes, keeping it a surprise was a dirty trick, but it also kept her reactions natural. The way her eyes widened in surprise, the way her lips parted. You couldn't fake those kinds of things.

She wasn't the only one caught by surprise though. The original plan was to share a quick peck on the cheek. Lewis hadn't counted on her mouth looking so alluring, nor had he anticipated how good her kiss would taste. Licking his lips, he swore he could still taste her sweetness.

Kisses didn't usually linger with him. In his mind, women were more or less interchangeable. Warm bodies that kept him from noticing he was alone. He wondered if the fact that this was his first sober kiss in a long time was the reason he found it so memorable. He'd been tempted to test the theory by kissing her again at the end of the night. But then, when they reached her doorstep and Susan looked up at him with those marvelous green-and-brown eyes…he'd backed away. Susan wasn't interchangeable. She deserved more respect than to be kissed simply for the sake of kissing.

But damn, he'd wanted to kiss her again. Wanted to so badly.

On the kitchen counter, his phone began buzzing an SOS signal, the vibration pattern he'd assigned Susan. He answered and hit Speaker while at the same time opening his refrigerator. "What can I do for you, Miss Collier?" he asked as he scanned the contents.

"Did your teammates really dislike you?"

"That's an odd way of starting a conversation," he replied. It appeared his housekeeper had done some grocery shopping for him. There was a fresh gallon of orange juice next to the milk.

"Did they?"

"I never spent enough time with them to know one way or another. Hung to myself mostly. Unless there was a party." He paused to take a swig of juice. "What's this about?"

"I'm sorry. Something my brother mentioned. He said you bounced from team to team because no one liked you."

"More like management disliked paying my heavy contract fees." Although he wasn't surprised to hear his bad-boy reputation had fueled different stories. Once again, his partying ways left their mark. "I take it your brother saw the paper."

"He did. He called you a degenerate."

"I've heard worse."

The pause on the other end of the line made him uneasy. "He's worried about scandal," Susan said. "I hadn't considered how this might affect the company. Collier's has only recently gotten back on solid footing. If people discover..."

"They won't. I promise. I'm going to be on my best behavior." He had too much to lose.

"I know you will," she replied.

Her faith surprised him. She was the first person he'd met who really believed he'd changed. "I don't want to put you in a bad spot. If you want to back out, I'll understand."

"I don't want to back out—I gave my word and I intend to keep it. Besides... I had a good time last night."

Lewis smiled at the shyness in her voice. "We're famous you know," he said.

"Everyone in my office is whispering and giving me looks. They probably don't think I've been kissed before."

"You have been, right?"

"Yes. Although never quite so publicly."

"You're not still sore about my keeping the Mistletoe Camera thing a secret, are you?"

The soft sigh on the other end of the line

sounded playfully exasperated. "I've recovered. But I want a promise that next time I'll get a little advance warning."

The memory of her glazed eyes popped into his head. "No worries there. I doubt there'll be a Mistletoe Cam at our next outing." Meaning he wouldn't have an excuse—that is, a reason—to kiss her.

"I suppose there wouldn't be, unless we were attending another basketball game. That's...good."

Was the clipped tone in her voice disappointment or relief? "I think so," he said. "I mean, it being a good thing. Can't go heavy on the PDA if I'm supposed to be changing my ways, right?"

"Right. Absolutely." He still couldn't tell. There was noise in the background. Maybe she was guarding her end of the conversation.

His ego took a little kick. A *little* disappointment would have been nice. It'd been a pretty decent kiss in his book. Heck, women were known to pull off their tops just to get his *attention*.

Those were women who wanted him though. Susan was with him as quid pro quo. She didn't really want him...

"Lewis?"

He shook his head. How long had he been staring into the neck of the orange juice bottle? "Did you say something?"

"I asked about the next step. Now that people know we're...that is, you know..."

"A couple," Lewis supplied. The word felt oddly normal.

"Exactly. What do we do now?"

Good question. According to his list, step two was to be seen at a few more formal events. Fundraisers with the proper people to establish his new social circle.

And he knew exactly the event. "How do you feel about the Kew Gardens?"

"In general? They're lovely. What does that have to do with us?"

"We're going to make our first official appearance there," Lewis told her. "This Saturday night. I hope you have a formal cocktail dress in your closet."

"I think I can rustle one up," she replied.

He had no doubt. "In the meantime, I'll talk to Michael about keeping up the momentum."

There was a pause on Susan's end of the line. He imagined her pretty pink lips drawing into a frown. "What does that mean?"

"Keeping us in the public eye, luv, of course," he said. "If all goes right, it'll be a fun week."

The next few days were unlike anything Susan had ever experienced. It was like she'd changed identities overnight.

"What's he like?" became a common question.

Along with "Is he as wild as they say?"

The photo from the basketball game—with help from Lewis's agent, no doubt—had set off a domino trail of publicity. A couple of local radio personalities had seen the story and it had become fodder for one of the morning talk show segments. That, of course, had led to more articles.

One, rehashing Lewis's past romantic rendezvous, she found uncomfortable to read. Another focused on her, with the article playing up the fact that she had ties not only to Collier's Soap, but to former sex kitten Belinda Quinn.

Thankfully, as she told Lewis, her mother was filming some island reality show in the middle of nowhere and was unreachable, saving them from having to deal with *that* particular crazy.

Susan felt like a rock star.

The best part? Courtney and Ginger were practically apoplectic with jealousy. Was it petty and childish of her to take pleasure in their envy? Yes, but she was enjoying it regardless.

The two women spent the first couple of days after the "Kiss-mas" article appeared whispering behind her back. Mostly disbelief that Susan was the woman Lewis had chosen to date.

Like he would have dated either one of you, Susan longed to say.

All right, given they were both gorgeous, Lewis probably would have dated them, but she bet he wouldn't have remembered their names. Lewis would always remember hers.

And Lewis had kissed her. It might have only been for the cameras, but it was still a kiss—something Courtney and Ginger couldn't claim.

It wasn't until Day Three that their whispers became more pointed. And louder.

"A friend of mine used to tend bar at Narcissus and he said his credit card was always getting turned down for lack of funds."

Susan was walking back to her office when she heard the comment. Glancing at the cubicle of her admin, Freema, she spied Ginger and Courtney hovering by the doorway. There was no doubt about whose credit card they meant.

"Ginger," she called over to them. The blonde's spine straightened the second she heard her name. "Shouldn't you be working on our upcoming media buys? You, too, Courtney?"

Two wide-eyed, gaping expressions greeted her. At least they had the good sense to be embarrassed over getting caught. "We, um… were just chatting," Courtney finally managed to spit out.

"Well, I suggest you save your chatting for your lunch hour and let Freema do her job. And…" Because she could, she took a couple steps closer for dramatic effect. "I'll remind you—once—that my personal life is none of your concern. Do I make myself clear?"

Ginger's red cheeks said it all. "Yes."

"Good. Because I don't want to have this talk again." Folding her arms, she stood and maintained steady eye contact until the two women moved away. As she was leaving, she swore she heard the word *Shrewsan* muttered under one of their breaths. Lunchtime would be quite the gossip session, she imagined.

Let them complain. She was a rock star.

* * *

A giant illuminated tunnel greeted the car as they pulled through the main gate at Kew Gardens a few nights later. As they passed beneath, Lewis heard Susan gasp. "Oh, my! This is amazing." Leaning forward in her seat, she looked upward. "It looks like something out of that sci-fi TV show where they enter the wormhole."

"It does at that," Lewis agreed. Hundreds of overhead lights twinkled all around them like stars. "You know what this means, don't you?"

She looked across the seat at him, the lights reflecting in her eyes. "What?"

"If the car starts shaking uncontrollably, abandon ship."

"Not in this dress I'm not."

If it were another woman, he would have started pretending to hit turbulence and saying *she's breaking up* in his best Scottish accent. She would have laughed and thought him rakishly charming, even if she were too young to get the reference.

Tonight however, he had a difficult enough time making any lame jokes. He was wound tighter than a drum. For Susan, this was just another event, but for him, it would be the first time he'd attended a black-tie event with the intention of staying and mingling. No signing autographs and blowing off early with a bootlegged bottle of whatever he could grab.

Susan's diamond earrings sparkled as she angled her head to look upward again. "I think they strung Christmas lights over the entire driveway," she said. "It looks absolutely magical."

It certainly did. Lewis had never been to Kew Gardens—nature walks weren't really his thing—but the Christmas lights were famous. "The flyer that came with the tickets did say we would be treated to a fantastical holiday light show. Guess they weren't kidding."

"What charity are we supporting anyway? I never thought to ask. Be embarrassing if I couldn't remember the names of my boyfriend's causes."

Lewis tensed. No one had ever referred to him by that word before. It unsettled him. More nerves, he decided. Susan was only joking.

"You shouldn't have too much trouble remembering," he told her. "It's for the Sports Trust for Children."

"Isn't that one of the prince's charities? You

don't believe in doing things small scale do you?"

"Wish I could tell you this was part of some grand strategy, but the truth is, I've been donating to the Sports Trust for years. Usually I give the tickets to this event away though."

"Why?"

"I'm not much for brie and crackers," he replied.

"No, I mean why the Sports Trust? In case someone asks," she said.

"Do people ask those sorts of questions?" Seeing how everyone in the room was a supporter, he would assume they didn't care.

"Never hurts to be prepared. What if I run into a reporter or some person on the board of directors? They might wonder why you all of a sudden decided to start attending boring cocktail parties. If we're smart, we'll have our stories straight. I don't want to scramble the way I had to with Thomas and Linus."

"You handled that situation well enough." Admirably actually. "But I see your point. In this case, you can tell people the truth. Football kept me off the streets. In fact, if it weren't for sports, God knows where I'd be." He wouldn't be attending charity cocktail parties, that's for sure. More likely he'd be working some dead-end job and trying to stay out of trouble. "Sports gives kids a way to escape and be kids, if only for a few hours. If my money can help a kid out of trouble then that's a good thing, right?"

"A very good thing," she replied.

He wasn't sure why, but her smile made him feel like he'd aced a test. It mattered that she knew he was capable of sincerity.

In keeping with the season, the Victorian greenhouse hosting the event was illuminated with soft pink-and-blue spotlights, giving the building a purple glow. Lewis directed their driver to pull into the valet line to let them out.

"I haven't been here since my grandfather took us as children," Susan said as they stepped onto the sidewalk.

"Puts you one up on me," Lewis replied. "I've never been."

He looked around at the rolling lawns. They looked lush and manicured, despite it being winter. The building itself was an astounding stretch of glass and metal, its doorway guarded by a set of robed statues. "Lot fancier than I expected," he said.

"I always assumed my memory of this place was distorted by childhood, but maybe not. If I remember correctly, this particular building was filled with all sorts of rare plants."

They followed the other guests up the granite steps to the entrance where they were welcomed by a pair of giant poinsettia towers and a whoosh of warm, moist air. It was like stepping into a giant tropical forest. Plants of every shape and size surrounded them.

"Smells like spring," Susan said.

Indeed. There was definitely a hint of fresh dirt to the air. A sharp contrast to the cold night air.

The coat check was in the corner, marked by a pair of ferns decorated with tiny Christmas ornaments. If he hadn't been looking for it, he might never have found it. He turned to Susan intending to help her with her coat only to find she'd already slipped the garment from her shoulders. His breath caught at the sight of her. She'd been waiting on her steps when he picked her up, so this was the first time he'd had a chance to see what she was wearing and the sight took his breath away. At the wedding, she'd gone for a retro look: black, white and tight. Tonight she had a more graceful look. Her pale pink dress had a gathered bodice and long flowy skirt. While the dress didn't hug her curves the way the dress at the wedding had, the outfit fit tightly enough to let people know she had a shape while the V-neck showed off her ample cleavage. He liked that her breasts were soft and natural looking too. He'd seen enough enhancements in his life to actually find them boring. In fact, he liked how everything about her looked soft and natural, right down to her hair which she let curl around her shoulders.

"You look great," he said.

Her skin turned the color of her dress. "Thanks. I don't go to a lot of formal events so I wasn't sure if this would work. I was afraid this might be too…" She paused as a woman in a sequined minidress and with mile-long legs sauntered by. "Dowdy."

"Nonsense. It suits you." Shoot. That sounded like he was saying dowdy suited her. "I mean, not everyone is the sequined-mini type."

"I'm certainly not, that's for sure," she said before adding in a lower voice, "Think I'd catch a cold baring that much skin."

"Skin is overrated. Seriously." She was giving him a look of disbelief. "I'm not saying I don't appreciate a miniskirt as much as the next guy, but there's something to be said about maintaining a little mystery, know what I mean?" He handed over their coats and waited for his claim ticket.

"Really? I always got the impression men wanted to get down to business as quickly as possible."

"Obviously, you've been hanging around the wrong type of man."

She blushed again. This time the color went past the V and the effect hit him square in the gut. He meant what he said. It was much more fun wondering how much of her very white skin was capable of blushing than seeing it from the start.

He reached out and twirled one of her curls around his index finger. "Trust me, luv. You look as good as anyone here. More so, even, because you've got class."

"And you are a very smooth talker, Mr. Matolo," she replied with a smile. "If things don't work out in the broadcast world, you can always get a job selling used cars. Come on, we've got mingling to do."

Lewis watched as she started along the leafy walkway. She didn't believe him, but it was true. She projected a level of class that came from years of breeding. Even when drunk at the wedding, she'd held herself with refinement. Lewis could barely muster it when he was sober. Sure, he had looks and charm, but at his core he was the little street kid being kicked from home to home. The one whom, if he hadn't been able to block a ball, wouldn't have been looked at twice by the people in Susan's world. The one who didn't belong...

"Are you coming?" Susan asked.

"One minute. Thought I'd enjoy the view a moment, first."

Score blush number three, although she tried to cover it with an exasperated eye roll. "Now you're just trying to get a rise out of me. If you really want a view, come check this out."

It was a Christmas jungle. In addition to the tropical plants, strategically placed Christmas trees dotted the walkway intersections. Each was decorated with a different color of the rainbow. Red. Orange. Yellow. Green. Blue. Violet. Only they weren't covered with traditional ornaments. Instead, silk butterflies and flowers mixed with the lights.

It wasn't the Christmas display that captured his attention, however. It was the dozens of men and women clustered around the display. All dripping with money and status.

A couple close to them turned in his direction, their gaze subtly looking them up and down. Judging. Whispering.

Suddenly he was that little boy again, waiting to be told he didn't belong.

"I need a drink," he said. He headed to the bar.

CHAPTER FIVE

Dɪᴅ ʜᴇ sᴀʏ he was getting a drink? Susan hurried after him, wishing her legs were longer so she could keep up. Amazing how the man could cut through a crowd like butter.

She finally caught up with him—nearly collided with him, actually—when he stopped cold about a foot from the bar. "What are you doing?"

"I—I…" He washed a hand across his lips. "Something stupid."

Exactly what she'd feared. The question was why? After all his talk about reforming his image, why would he risk sabotaging himself right as his plan was taking off?

There were too many people around to have this conversation. Lewis's arrival had most of the room starstruck. She could see people all around them sneaking glances.

Grabbing his hand, she moved past the bar

and down the back pathway where she spied a water display in the far corner. The splashing water from the falls discouraged most people from standing too close. They would have privacy there.

There was only one other couple lingering by the water's edge. The pair shot them a look upon arrival, with the woman, not surprisingly, looking a bit incredulously at Susan. Ignoring them, Susan pulled Lewis off the walkway and into the foliage. There was only a small spot of bare ground, but if they stood close together, they wouldn't trample anything. "What are you doing, Lewis?" she hissed, just loud enough to be heard over the water. "I thought you were a 'changed man.' Pretty sure making a beeline for the bar isn't one of the sobriety rules. And don't try to tell me you meant to grab a glass of water, because I saw the look on your face." It was like a mask had dropped over his features. The muscles by his jaw began to twitch.

He wore a different expression now. Eyes lowered, his brow drawn together. "I know. It was stupid. I wasn't thinking."

Something had flipped his switch. "People don't just fall off the wagon without some kind of trigger. What happened?"

He shook his head. "It doesn't matter."

"Yes, it does matter," she told him. "I didn't agree to this little charade only to have you muck it up and embarrass us both."

Plus, not that she'd say so out loud, his sudden change in demeanor worried her. He was supposed to be this sexy, confident "reformed" playboy. The man she saw a moment ago had looked vulnerable and dare she say, insecure. Insecurity was *her* albatross. Men with perfect faces and perfect lips didn't experience self-doubt.

"You don't have to worry," Lewis told her. "It was a momentary blip. Nothing more."

"I believe you." After all, he'd stopped himself before even getting to the bar. "Still, I'd feel better if I knew what set the blip off."

"Silly really," he said, looking downward. "I've faced down some of the world's toughest players with thousands of people watching without flinching, but put me in a room full of tuxedo-wearing strangers and I'm a bundle of nerves." Susan's breath caught as he moved his hand toward her shoulder, only to fiddle with a frond hanging behind her. "I'm sure that sounds ludicrous to someone like you."

"What do you mean *someone like me*?" The branch he was playing with was brushing against her curls, causing little ripples of awareness.

"This is your world. Sophisticated. High-brow. You belong in it."

Hardly, but this wasn't the time to argue. At least about that. "Excuse me, Mr. Celebrity Millionaire. This is your world too."

"You know," he said, "I tell myself that very thing all the time. That I belong."

"But?" She could hear the doubt in his voice.

"But then I look at these people and I can hear them thinking *What is he doing here?* It's like they know where I came from."

"So what if they do?" she asked. "You have nothing to be ashamed of. Heck, half of this room is probably wondering how they can wrangle an introduction. More than half, likely."

"For now."

Susan frowned. "I don't understand."

"You said it yourself. I'm a celebrity. The more distance between me and my playing days, however, the less it'll matter. Until eventually I'll be just some bloke who was once a somebody and they'll wonder..." He shook his head. "Never mind."

"Tell me. Please." If whatever was on his

mind was distressing enough that he would consider drinking, she wanted to help.

He answered so softly, she almost didn't hear. "And they'll wonder why they ever wanted me around in the first place. Silly, huh?"

A piece of her heart broke for him. "No," she told him. Illogical perhaps, but far from silly. He wasn't talking about reality; he was talking about a feeling that dwelled deep down inside a person. A feeling logic couldn't always touch.

"The Collier men are all very tall," she told him. "Very tall, very handsome and very charismatic, like my father. My mother is very beautiful. Like stop-traffic beautiful."

He was looking at her with dark, fathomless eyes. "I'm not following."

"When I was seven or eight—right before my mother took off—my parents threw a party. I wore this fancy party dress and my father told me how pretty I looked. I asked if I was as pretty as Mommy. And when he replied, *Absolutely*, my mother replied, *Don't lie to the girl, Preston*. That was the moment I knew that I wasn't like the rest of them. No matter how hard I tried, I would always be the odd one out."

Now it was she who felt judged as Lewis's gaze bore down on her. She'd meant the example as a sign of solidarity. Instead, she'd revealed that she was the Ugly Duckling of her family. He must think her daft. Why did she share anything?

His deep brown eyes moved closer. "Thank you. Knowing you understand means a lot." He ran the back of his hand down her cheek. "More than you could know."

A shiver worked its way through Susan's body. Odd, since she'd suddenly grown very warm. Between the greenhouse temperature and the warmth emanating from Lewis's body, the air around her had grown thick. It was making her light-headed.

"Everything all right?" Lewis asked.

"Can we sit down somewhere?"

"Of course. Come with me." He tucked a curl behind her ear.

Since the other couple had departed—escaping the awkwardness of standing near a couple whispering in the bushes no doubt— Susan assumed they would head back to the walkway. Instead, Lewis took her hand and together they picked their way toward the waterfall.

"You were looking a little pink," he said,

as he guided her to a seat on a nearby rock. The air was noticeably cooler by the water.

"We're going to get in trouble for being off the walkway."

"We won't stay long. Besides, the gardeners or whatever walk through here, don't they? That's why there are paths."

Susan shook her head. "You're funny. One minute you're telling me you worry about fitting in and the next you're flouting the rules. One would think you're self-sabotaging."

"Psychoanalyzing again, are we?"

"I told you, psychology's my thing." Fat lot of good it ever did her though. Being able to psychoanalyze everyone but herself.

"Bit of an odd hobby, isn't it?" Lewis asked.

"What can I say? I'm rubbish at arts and crafts. I got into it when I was a teenager. My attempt to understand my mother better."

He touched her knee, his hand bringing a steadying warmth. "Did you? Understand her better?"

"I learned a bunch of terms, all of which boiled down to her being a selfish piece of work who didn't want to share the spotlight with a child. They want so much attention, you know."

She tossed aside the last part with an

overdramatic voice, but the sting never really left. When she was younger she blamed her looks, thinking if she was taller or thinner or elegant like the Collier boys, then her mother might have wanted her around. As she grew older, however, she realized her mother wouldn't have wanted the competition. The sad truth was her mother just plain didn't want her.

"At least you knew how she felt," Lewis said. "My mum cried holy hell when they took me away, but not so much that she couldn't get her act together."

"Just like Belinda," she said. "Guess that makes us two odd peas in a pod."

"Guess so," Lewis replied with a smile.

She slipped her hand over his, and their fingers entwined. With the connection came a strange, full kind of feeling. Kinship, Susan realized. For the first time she felt understood. It was a heady, seductive feeling.

Ironic that she would set out to comfort him and end up being the one comforted.

"I'm not the only one who's an enigma," he continued.

"What do you mean?"

"Well, for one thing, I keep looking for this unlikable shrew part of you, and I can't see it. I mean, you've got sharp edges, but who hasn't, right?"

He couldn't have said a nicer thing if he tried. "Thank you."

"Just calling it like I see it. And what I see looks pretty nice. Very nice, in fact." His smile sobered as his gaze dropped to her lips. Susan's pulse quickened, remembering the last time he'd looked at her mouth.

Instead of leaning in like she thought he would, however, Lewis suddenly released her hand and rose to his feet.

"We should get back on the path before we get in trouble," he said. "Won't do either of our reputations any good if we get tossed out on our ears. I can see the headline now. Stay Off the Grass, Lewis!"

"I'm sure they'd come up with something punnier than that." Although an example escaped her. She was too busy hiding her disappointment behind smoothing her dress. Her embarrassment too, for thinking he'd been about to kiss her. Talk about foolish. There were no cameras, no giant screen. Why would he want to kiss her if there was nothing to gain?

They snuck out of the plants the way they'd come, emerging to the backs of several other partygoers who were standing on the path.

"And here we thought we were being so sneaky. I bet half the party saw us." She looked over at Lewis who was smoothing the front of his jacket. He looked as crisp and elegant as before.

"If they did, no one would say anything," he said. "My guess? They didn't care."

"Or they were too polite to make a scene with photographers about." She and Lewis might have joked about negative headlines, but in reality, the sponsors of the event wouldn't want the bad press.

"Either way, we lucked out then, didn't we? Come on, I'll buy you a glass of champagne before we mingle. I don't suppose you know anyone here?"

Other than one or two faces she recognized from Collier's functions, not really. Since attending solo wasn't much fun, she only went to charity events when Linus needed an emergency date, which wasn't often. She didn't want to tell him that though, because it would reveal how pathetic her social life was. This faux romance was the most social activity she'd had in who knows how long.

"Excuse me, Mr. Matolo?"

They'd managed to go no more than a handful of steps before they were stopped by a pair of official-looking gentlemen. The younger of the two reminded Susan of a thinner, nerdier version of the Duke of Sussex with red hair and a neatly trimmed goatee. The other resembled an owl. Rotund with tortoiseshell glasses and an extremely receding hairline.

It was the younger one who addressed them. "I'm Christopher Redmayne, from the Sports Trust for Children and this is Graham Montclark."

She felt Lewis's body stiffen from six inches away. "As in Montclark Communications?" he asked. Montclark was Britain's largest private media corporation. "I believe I've read your name atop a scoreboard or two."

The balding man didn't return Lewis's smile. "I'm sure you have. The company sponsors several sporting venues."

"The two of us have been waiting for you to step away from the water display," Redmayne said.

So much for escaping comment. "I'm sorry about that," she said. "I—"

"Susan was feeling a bit light-headed. I thought the air might be cooler by the water." Lewis clasped her hand and squeezed. "Didn't want her keeling over or anything. I hope that wasn't a problem?"

"No, of course not," Redmayne replied. If it was a problem, Lewis's explanation coupled with the fear of a guest fainting kept him from saying so. "Are you feeling better, Ms...?"

"Collier, and yes. Thank you. Lewis knew exactly what I needed. In fact, he was just about to get me something cold to drink."

"Good. Good," Redmayne replied. "A cold drink is always a good idea."

Interestingly though, the two men didn't make a move to step aside or leave. They remained planted in the middle of the path, apparently intent on having a conversation.

"Collier," Montclark said. "Any relation to Thomas?"

"My brother."

The businessman nodded. "Good man. Miraculous story, that business with his wife."

"Yes. The whole family was shocked when she returned. In a good way of course. We like to think of it as a true Christmas miracle."

"Graham is one of our advisors. I was telling him how generous you've been to our organization," Redmayne said. "Your support is very appreciated. It's always a surprise, to see who is willing to step up and help."

"You do good work," Lewis replied. "Why wouldn't I support you?"

"That's nice to hear." At that moment, a server walked by carrying a tray of champagne. Holding up a hand, Redmayne stopped the man from passing. "Could you get a glass of water for Ms. Collier?" he asked.

"Actually… Champagne will be fine." This conversation defined the term awkward. If it was going to continue, she would need more than water.

"I'll take the water, if you don't mind," Lewis said. You could tell both of the other men were struggling not to look surprised. "I'm a teetotaler these days."

Susan smiled at him with pride. The admission couldn't have been easy for him. Not in this environment where he already felt judged.

Redmayne recovered first, with the grace one expected from an experienced networker. "I should take a page from your book. Every holiday I swear I'm going to cut back on excesses and every year I'm filled with regret because my pants are too snug." The four of them shared an uncomfortable chuckle.

"Anyway," Redmayne continued, "I hate to talk business when the two of you are here to enjoy yourselves, but we're hosting a Christmas event for our young ambassadors on December eleventh. Heath Chilton was supposed to lead a sports clinic but we found out this morning that he's having a second knee surgery and won't be able to attend so…"

"You're wondering if Lewis would be able to step in!" In a voice suiting a loyal girlfriend, Susan finished the sentence for him. Actually she suspected Redmayne wanted to ask if Lewis could use his contacts to get a current player—hence the awkwardness—and she jumped in to get Lewis's name on the table first. From the look Redmayne shared with Montclark, it was a good thing she had. "I think that's a terrific idea. Lewis was just saying how he wanted to get more involved with the program. Weren't you?"

He picked up her train of thought immediately. "Yes, I was, and I'd be honored to step in."

Redmayne was scrambling for a polite way to escape the hole he was in. "That's very generous of you, but, um…" He looked at Montclark, who opened his mouth to finish.

Lewis cut them off. "In fact," he said, "I

know what Heath charges for public appearances. If it would help the organization's bottom line, I would be glad to donate my time free of charge."

Well done. Susan smiled into her champagne. A light gleamed in Montclark's eyes. The idea of saving a sizable amount of money clearly appealed to him. "We're looking to inspire these kids. Can we count on you to show up, ready to perform?"

"Mr. Montclark, I always show up ready to play," Lewis told him. "You have my word."

The reassurance didn't seem to impress the businessman, but the organization had its back against the wall. That they'd approached Lewis for any kind of assistance this close to the event said they were desperate. Susan knew what the two men were thinking. A free-of-charge, former player was better than no player at all.

The waiter returned with Lewis's water. "Here's your water, Mr. Matolo," he said. Servers probably didn't usually address the guests by name but the young man's starstuck expression as well as the excited tremor in his voice explained the break in protocol.

"Thanks, mate. Appreciate it."

Tucking the tray under his arm, the young

man prepared to leave only to pause. "I've watched every game you ever played in."

"Wow," Lewis replied. "What'd you do? Start watching when you were in diapers?"

Susan watched Montclark taking in the exchange, particularly the waiter's starstuck face. After a few minutes more of conversation—and a request for a selfie—the young man moved on and Montclark cleared his throat. "Very well," he said, "since you are willing to make a firm commitment and waive your appearance fee…"

"Anything to help the organization," Lewis replied.

"We appreciate you stepping up on such short notice. Redmayne will send your agent all the information." The three men shook on the arrangement.

"Remind me to tip that server extra," Susan said once Redmayne and Montclark had moved on to the buffet table. "His timing couldn't have been more perfect if we paid him." There was no doubt his enthusiasm was what had finally convinced Montclark.

"Should I tip you too?" Lewis asked.

"Beg your pardon?"

"For backing them into the corner in the first place. We both know they wanted to use my connections, not hire me. If you hadn't jumped in with the idea, it never would have come up."

"You wanted to rehab your image. What better way than to dazzle them with your newfound dedication to charity?"

"Not to mention impressing Graham Mont-clark."

"Oh, do his stations carry the matches? I hadn't realized." Putting a hand to her chest, she blinked with false innocence.

Lewis chuckled, his accompanying smile devilishly crooked. "Well played, Ms. Collier. I knew I picked the right woman."

His words had the smoothness of raw honey dripping from a spoon. They ran through her, leaving a slow warmth.

He means the right woman for the arrangement.

She needed a dose of reality to counteract the sweetness. None of this was real. She'd be wise to keep that in mind before she did something incredibly stupid.

Like fall for the man.

CHAPTER SIX

LEWIS HAD DATED a lot of women in his adult life. Too many really. None of them, though, were like Susan. Granted, that was the point, but never had he thought that different would be so interesting.

They were on their way home, still in character, as it were. He had his arm slung across the back seat while Susan sat close to his side. Not overly close, and certainly not draped across his lap like a lot of his dates. Susan was far too classy for that kind of behavior.

Susan was a lot of things. She was smart and sophisticated, not to mention perceptive. When he had freaked out, she'd known exactly what to say.

An odd experience, it was, being understood. When she touched his hand, the warmth shot straight through him, the sensation simultaneously comforting and terrifying.

He wasn't used to sharing pieces of himself. Better to maintain distance, he always said. It made leaving easier. With Susan, however— and maybe it was because they were so alike— with Susan, sharing felt normal.

The car turned a corner. In spite of the late hour, there were plenty of lights on. Some of the windows already had candles and in one or two, he spied Christmas trees. "Early birds," he murmured.

"Who are early birds?" Susan asked. When she turned to look at him, he caught a whiff of vanilla shampoo. Reminded him of cookies.

"The trees," he replied. "Some people already have theirs up. They're early birds."

"Probably the same people who start playing Christmas music the day after Halloween and have their shopping done a month early."

"I'm going to go out on a limb and guess that you aren't one of those people."

"Definitely not." Even in the dark he could see her eyes widen in horror. Whether she realized it or not, her little protest had shifted her closer to him. Her shoulder brushed against the edge of his coat. "No shopping until December first. That's my rule."

Lewis looked at his watch. "Good news

then. You can start officially start shopping. It's after midnight."

"Huzzah! I'll fire up my computer as soon as I get home."

"That's the Christmas spirit." Unable to help himself, he wrapped his arm around her shoulder and squeezed, pulling her body into the crook of his arm as he did so. He liked that she was huggable. When you pulled her close, her body was warm and comfortable. The kind of body built for cuddling.

He'd never been one for cuddling before.

"I don't know what I would have done without you tonight," he said. "You were brilliant."

Despite the shadows, he could feel she was blushing. "I told you before, you played as big a part in convincing Montclark as I did. If you really want to thank someone, thank the waiter."

"Man's timing *was* impeccable." It was Susan, though, who made him feel confident. "I don't think I would have made it through the entire party if you hadn't been there to talk me off the ledge."

"Don't be silly. You righted yourself all on your own," she said.

Perhaps, but her gentle reassurance was

what had kept him righted from that moment on. "The stories you shared…"

Her gaze fell away. "Who knew sharing my childhood angst would be so powerful?"

"Don't sell yourself short." They both knew the real meaning behind her story. She'd peeled back a layer of herself to let him know he wasn't alone. That she, in her own way, understood how it felt to be on the outside looking in.

For as long as he could remember, he'd been left of center. Separate and alone, even when surrounded by people. Oh, he put on a good face, but in the end that's all it was, a face. Even when he was part of a team, he never truly felt a sense of solidarity. Why bother when you were only going to move on?

But tonight, he didn't feel alone. He and Susan were a team. The idea was headier than anything he ever felt. It took his breath away, and at the same time, scared him. He didn't do close. He did self-preservation.

Regardless, she deserved to know just how much her honesty meant to him. "All that stuff I told you tonight…" He chose his words carefully in case the driver was listening. "I've never told anyone before."

Her breath caught, and a second later her head came to rest on his shoulder. "Me neither," she said.

"Your apartment is right ahead, miss," the driver said.

His announcement was a switch, ending the moment. Almost immediately, the two of them straightened, with Susan shifting one way and Lewis the other. The gap that formed was imperceptible, but Lewis's side grew cooler nevertheless.

He busied himself with watching the traffic while Susan fiddled with her bag and the driver parallel parked.

"Tonight was fun."

At the sound of Susan's voice, he turned his head. "I'm glad you enjoyed yourself."

"I did. Between this and the basketball game, you've set the bar pretty high. Makes me wonder what you'll come up with next."

"You'll have to wait and see."

The driver opened the door, and they stepped onto the sidewalk.

"Should I wait?" the driver asked.

"I... No. I'll be right back," he replied. "I have an early morning tomorrow."

Ignoring what looked like a flash of disappointment flaring in Susan's eyes, Lewis guided her up the walkway to the red door marking the entrance to her apartment building. "If you give me your keys, I'll open the door for you."

"I think I can handle a key," she replied before reaching into her bag and pulling out a large key ring. "It's hardly complicated."

"Yes, but the driver is watching. Since we don't know if he'll try to sell us out, I should make a point of unlocking and walking you in the door."

"Absolutely. We've got to keep up appearances, don't we? However, the front door has a keypad. The lock is for my apartment door."

There it was again, that distance, and he couldn't figure out why. Nothing he had said seemed inappropriate. "All right then, why don't you give me the key code."

"Fine," she said with a sigh.

As he punched in the numbers, Lewis fought the urge to turn around and check on the driver who might or might not be paying attention.

No sooner had he opened the door, than Susan started over the threshold.

"Wait." He grabbed her wrist to keep her from disappearing. "I need to kiss you goodnight. The driver might be watching. We want to give him something he can peddle to Lorianne or another columnist."

"Right," she replied. "We want to give the right impression."

Lewis couldn't tell if the sarcasm in her voice was meant to be humorous or not. With the shadows obscuring her expression, it was impossible to tell. It didn't matter though. Appearances needed to be maintained. Slipping his arm around her waist, he closed the space between them and kissed her. Just as he had at the game, he only intended a brief, chaste peck. The moment his lips touched hers, however, any thought of chaste flew out the window.

Her mouth was made for kissing. Their lips slanted together like links in a chain, Susan's mouth yielding without urging. Her head fell back and her body arched against him. Lewis's body, still humming with awareness from earlier, reacted immediately. Pulling her close, he pressed his hips to hers, delivering a deep, soulful kiss while his free hand tangled in her curls.

Susan's eyes were glazed when they finally broke apart, or so he told himself. Again, he couldn't see her expression, but since *he* was dazed, he hoped she was, as well. From one kiss. His body was on full alert now, wanting nothing more than to take her upstairs and continue.

Fortunately common sense had maintained a tenuous grip, and he was able to step back. "Continuing" wasn't part of their deal.

Taking a breath, he stepped backward again, down to the step below. "Well, that should give the driver some gossip to peddle," he said.

Hopefully his grin didn't look as shaky as it felt.

"I think it's time we slept together."

Susan tripped over a crack in the sidewalk and nearly dropped her coffee. It was three weeks into their "relationship," and they were spending the weekend afternoon Christmas shopping. Until now, they'd stuck to highly visible social events where their status as a couple was documented by official photographers and social reporters. Lewis felt the timing was such that they should embark on Step Three of his plan, or what he called "doing coupley things." His agent said he would tip off the tabloids that the two of them would be spending the day on Regent Street on the off chance they wanted to snag a photo of the budding romance.

At the moment, the only thing they'd snag would be a shot of her staring at him bug-eyed.

"Not literally, obviously," Lewis said catching her elbow.

No, of course not. Susan focused on adjusting her jacket so he wouldn't see her disappointment. Sleeping together didn't involve an audience, and Lewis didn't initiate any displays of affection unless someone was watching.

How could he turn his emotions on and off like that? All gentle touches and intimate glances in public only to back away the moment they were alone. They'd even taken to stepping inside the doorway of her building to say goodbye so he wouldn't have to kiss her goodnight.

Clearly she'd been a little too enthusiastic in her response the other night. Honestly, what did he expect though after essentially telling her she was special on the drive home?

Then again, maybe the admission had been for show too. They hadn't been alone.

Recovering herself, she made a show of taking a sip of coffee. "What would be the point of pretending we're sleeping together?" she asked. Besides frustrating her.

"Because people expect to see a real relationship move forward. It's the twenty-first century. People in serious relationships sleep together."

"I know that." She may not have had a serious love affair in her lifetime, but she had dated people for more than a few months. "I mean, what would be the overall goal? We'd get a blind item saying you spent the night or a pic in the *Looking Glass* of us heading out to breakfast?"

"You got a better idea?"

"Not really, but..."

She'd been thinking about this a lot the past few days. There was a hole in Lewis's plan. "Blind items aren't read by everyone. There's no guarantee your message is going to reach the people you need to influence. Same with attending a few social events." The more she thought, the more she wondered if their plan was a waste of time.

Or maybe it was that the phoniness of it all was beginning to chafe. Tipping off photographers, pretending for witnesses. Every gimmick was a reminder that she wasn't good enough to be a real girlfriend.

It wouldn't be so bad if he weren't so damn amazing when they were together. Like today when he'd shown up on her doorstep bearing coffee for their shopping adventure. He even tucked in her scarf under the guise of keeping her warm while they walked. All for the benefit of anyone who might be watching.

Why wasn't she worthy of such treatment in private? Susan sighed. When she agreed to play along, it was so people like Courtney and Ginger would stop calling her pathetic. Now she wondered if she was merely proving them right.

"Earth to Susan…" A leather glove waved in her face. "You there?"

"Sorry," she replied. "You were saying?"

"I was saying you're right. We need to make a bigger splash. I'll talk to Michael about scoring a profile article in one of the weekly mags. How do you feel about becoming a cover model?"

Awkward. "Who on earth would want to read an article about me?"

"I would. You're a fascinating woman." His smile made her stomach tumble. There he went again, making her feel special. "But I'm thinking about a profile about both of us. One of those 'How Love Saved Me' articles. What do you think?"

Terrific. So not only did he want to take their fake romance to the next fake level, he wanted to give an interview about how much he fake loved her. The idea gave her heartburn. "I think I need to check your coffee," she said.

"Nothing but Italian roast, I swear. Here, do you want to test it?" He held out the cup.

Susan pushed it back. "I'll take your word for it."

"The more I think about it," Lewis continued, "the more I can't believe I didn't think of the idea sooner. A feature article would convince people a lot faster and it would give Collier's some good publicity, as well."

"I didn't realize you were in a rush," she said.

"I'm not looking to dawdle—the season will be starting soon enough."

"You're going to have to hustle if you want to be featured before the holidays," she said. "Even weekly magazines have a lead time. Too close to the holidays, and you'll have to keep up the ruse through January. We only mapped out an agreement through the holidays, so unless you want to extend things…"

"I'll call Michael first thing on Monday morning," he said. "I don't want to tie you up longer than necessary."

What he really meant was tie him up. The sooner he established himself as a reliable potential commentator, the sooner he could go about finding a woman who was more his type. She swallowed the bad taste that suddenly filled her mouth.

No sense dwelling on the inevitable. They had nearly a month to go before they parted company. Today was about "being coupley."

"Is there a game plan for this shopping expedition or are we just going to parade up and down the street letting people stare at us?" she asked.

"Up to you. I'm more of an online shopper myself."

"How personal."

"How convenient," Lewis replied. "One click and you're done."

Susan wondered if she was part of his "one click." They'd decided they weren't spending Christmas together. Did fake couples bother to exchange gifts if they weren't being watched?

Stop whining. You knew what you were getting into.

"As much as I enjoy people staring, I think we should do something. Do you feel up to tackling a toy store? My niece Maddie wants Bugnoculars."

"Bug-what?"

The way he scrunched up his face in confusion was adorable. "Binoculars that let you look at bugs close up," she explained. Her niece had become a budding entomologist. "Actually, she wants two pairs. One for her and one for her stuffed pet, Bigsby. Oh, and a kitten too, but I was informed she's already put in an order for the animal with Santa."

"Hope for her sake, he comes through."

"Last year she asked for a visit from her dead mother, and got her wish. A 'gray tiger kitten with a red bow' shouldn't be too difficult, considering."

Naturally her sister-in-law's reappearance at Christmastime was merely coincidence, but Maddie believed it was all Santa. Susan saw no sense bursting her bubble. In a few years the little girl would learn the truth about Santa and that part of her innocence would die forever. "How old were you when you stopped believing in Santa?" she asked.

"Six," Lewis replied. "I told one of the other kids at the foster home that Santa was bringing me a race car set, and he let me know the score."

Six years old. It saddened her, thinking of how disappointed he must have been.

"Wouldn't you know, *his* mom got her act

together for the holidays and showed up with the exact set I wanted. I got to watch him and his brother play with the thing all day."

She didn't dare ask about Lewis's mother, suspecting she knew the answer. "Didn't they let you join them?"

"Nah. Wasn't part of the family," he said, eyes looking off in the distance. In that moment, his profile looked so forlornly beautiful it made her throat clutch. She squeezed her coffee cup to keep from pulling him into a hug. Lewis shook his head. "I was too young." Maybe she was projecting, but his offhand comment came out flat. "What about you," he asked. "When did you figure it out?"

"Fourth grade." She remembered well. "My classmates told me. Turned out I was the only one who was still a believer. The whole class got quite a laugh." The memory of her embarrassment swirled in her stomach. "Oh, well," she said. "Whatever. It was a long time ago. I've recovered."

"My resilient little pea?"

His what? Right, they were two odd peas in a pod. Was it strange that whenever they shared sad childhood tales, she ended up feeling warm from the inside out?

She decided to change the subject before

things became too maudlin. "Hamleys is only a block away. Ready to tackle the crowds?"

Breaching the gap between them, Lewis took her arm and tucked it in the crook of his own. "Crowds are what we want, luv. Remember?"

Good thing too because it was the opening weekend of Santa's grotto. As a result, the toy store was filled with children dressed in their Christmas finery waiting to go upstairs for their chance to speak with the man himself while their parents snapped a photo for the annual Christmas card. If ever there would be a place where they'd be noticed, this was it. Most of the kids would be too young to recognize Lewis, but their parents weren't. Susan saw a number of heads turn in their direction as they walked in.

"I think the science toys are on the second floor," Susan told him.

She made it halfway to the staircase before she realized Lewis wasn't following. Figuring someone must have stopped him for an autograph or photo, she turned and scanned the crowd. It wasn't difficult to find his tall form in the crowd and she soon spied him by the animatronic display. The store was famous for its fantastical panoramas. This year, the wall was a winter resort with animals of all sorts enjoying the great outdoors. Teddy bears rode a ski lift. A pair of rabbits were ice skating on a pond. There was even a cut-out of a lodge where a sloth lay stretched in a hammock by a roaring fire.

Lewis was mesmerized. His eyes were wide and shining and he had an almost slack-jawed look of wonder about him. Maddie wore a similar look when Susan had brought her last year. Lewis's expression caused warmth to spread through her chest. He looked beautiful when his guard slipped. She wanted to wrap her arms around him and soak him up.

Suddenly it hit her. He was viewing the display with a child's eye for good reason. "You've never been in here at Christmastime, have you?" she asked.

"Never been in here period," he replied. "No reason to."

And probably too far away when he was a child. How much childhood had he lost moving from home to home? While she was the odd person out in her family, she at least had one. Her heart ached picturing the little boy watching his foster siblings play with the toy he wished for. It wasn't just the toy that caused the pain; it was being shut out.

Without giving it a second thought, she wrapped her arms around his biceps and rested a head on his shoulder. Her way of saying he wasn't frozen out anymore. The shifting of muscles beneath her cheek told her Lewis had looked down in surprise, but he didn't say a word.

"Pretty amazing, isn't it?" she remarked. "It must take them months to plan everything out. All the little details."

Lewis chuckled. "There's a red squirrel dancing in one of the trees. I had a teammate who danced like that. Hector Menendez. Called it his booty dance. I should send him a video to show him how awkward he looked." He took out his phone.

Susan was watching another set of rabbits, this pair chasing one another around a tree trunk. "My grandfather used to bring us here when we were little."

"Same one who took you to the Kew Gardens?"

Susan nodded. "He took us a lot of places. The company museum was his favorite—always a good time."

"Didn't like learning about soap?"

"Thomas and Linus liked it. I was four years old. I just wanted ice cream. Come to think of it, there are days when I'd still rather eat ice cream than be at Collier's. For that matter, I'd take ice cream over anything."

"Anything?" Lewis asked. Actually he purred, making her insides flip. "I can think of a few things I might like better."

There must be someone nearby watching because he had his nose dangerously close to her temple. Very well. She'd play along. "Is that so? Like what?"

"Sugar cookies, for starters."

Susan nearly snorted. That was so not what she expected. But then, this was a show, not a seduction. Why shouldn't he give a nonsensical answer? "Cookies over ice cream? Close call, but I don't think so."

"That's your opinion. Lately I've been finding the aroma very tempting. Has anyone ever told you that you have gorgeous hair?"

The non sequitur threw her, along with a brush across the top of her head that felt a lot like a kiss.

For the crowd.

"I've gotten a few compliments," she replied.

In reality, her hair was a source of vanity for her. She had the Collier black hair, one of the few family traits—maybe the only family trait—from that side of the family that had been passed down to her.

"Good. Glad to hear it didn't go unnoticed."

Like the rest of her, she almost said. Instead, she whispered, "Thank you," and, closing her eyes, rested her cheek a little more firmly against his woolen coat.

"Did you know your hair smells like sugar cookies?" Lewis whispered back.

Susan's eyes flew open. Pulling back, she looked at him expecting a grin. He was dead serious though. If anything, his eyes were slightly hooded. "Your shampoo," he said. "Reminds me of sugar cookies."

He just said he preferred sugar cookies. Was he trying to say…

The sound of her phone interrupted her thoughts before they could become coherent. Pulling her phone from her bag, she saw her brother Linus's face on the caller ID.

"Might want to head to the hospital," he said when she answered. "Baby number two has arrived."

CHAPTER SEVEN

"THE BABY'S HERE! The baby's here!" Susan's niece nearly lifted off the ground, propelling herself into her aunt's arms. A wispy little live wire she was, bouncing up and down on her toes even as she hugged Susan's midsection. "I'm a big sister," she announced in a loud, proud voice.

"And everyone in the hospital knows," Susan replied. "You need to keep your voice down though, so you won't wake the babies in the nursery."

Lewis watched the moment unfold from a few feet away. They stood outside one of the birthing suites in the maternity ward having hurried over as soon as Linus had called. He noticed Susan wore a giant smile as she admonished the girl, a clear indication she didn't really mind the boisterous greeting. She pressed one hand to her niece's back, while the other gently smoothed her bobbed brown hair. Even if she hadn't told him how much she adored Maddie, he'd have known from the tender expression on her face.

She knelt down so she was eye level with the girl. "Do you have a brother or a sister?"

"Brother. His name is No-Well."

"That would be Noel." A man joined them. Judging from his lanky frame, Lewis assumed it was one of Susan's brothers. Linus, the middle one, most likely. He looked too laid-back to be a new father. "She read the name card on the bassinet and thinks he's named after the Christmas song," he said. "Noel Christopher Collier."

"Got a bit of a Christmas theme going there, don't they?" The remark was out of his mouth before he could catch it.

Susan didn't seem to mind. In fact, she laughed. "My brother and his wife have a thing about Christmas. They think some kind of Christmas magic brought them back together."

Whatever floats their boat. Someone needed to believe in Christmas miracles.

He listened while Susan peppered her brother with questions about the baby's weight and other pertinent details.

"When did she go into labor?" she asked.

"Middle of the night, from what Thomas said. I'm not too clear on the details. Maddie was with the housekeeper when I picked her up."

"You weren't home," Maddie said. "We called you."

"I'm sorry, sweetheart. I didn't hear the phone. I was out Christmas shopping."

"With a friend," Linus noted. He'd finally acknowledged Lewis's presence. A pair of extremely intelligent blue eyes looked him up and down. "Hello."

There was definitely scrutiny in the greeting. As well as a good dose of protectiveness. Lewis's eyes darted to Susan who blushed and looked away. Lewis couldn't blame the man. If he had a sister and thought she was dating someone like him, he'd scrutinize the guy too.

"Lewis Matolo," he said, extending his hand. "Pleased to meet you."

"Linus Collier. Likewise." If he was insincere, the man's smile didn't show it. "Sorry to interrupt your shopping date."

"No problem. We can shop anytime. It's not every day someone has a baby."

"I'm Maddie." The little girl had her hand

out, mimicking her uncle. When Lewis accepted, she yanked his arm up and down with enthusiasm. Had she been an adult, he would have popped an elbow.

"Hello, Maddie," he said. "Congratulations on your baby brother."

"I'm getting a kitten too. Santa's bringing him," she replied before tilting her head and switching gears in the way only children could. "Are you Aunt Susan's boyfriend? Uncle Linus says you are."

Lewis's cheeks grew warm. He wasn't expecting the third degree from a six-year-old. "I…um…" From his place behind his niece, Susan's brother was waiting for his response.

Susan stepped in before he could answer. "Lewis is a very good friend," she said. "He was helping me pick out your Christmas present."

"Really?" Maddie's eyes widened. "What did you get?"

"We can't tell you that," Lewis replied. "It would spoil the surprise."

"Aunt Susan says surprises are overrated."

"Yes, I know. She told me how she felt about them when we went to a basketball game recently." Susan ducked her head to hide her pinking cheeks. Lewis waited until she glanced at him through her lashes and then he grinned.

The exchange didn't escape her brother who scrutinized them both. "I'm sure Aunt Susan meant unpleasant surprises," Linus said. "Not good surprises like presents."

"Absolutely," Susan answered. "Some surprises are definitely worth waiting for. Like Christmas presents. So you're just going to have to wait, little munchkin."

"Okay." Maddie's disappointed expression didn't look very permanent. In fact, the frown disappeared about a second after it appeared, in correlation with the suite's door opening up.

"Daddy!" the little girl bounced away from Susan and toward the dark-haired man who'd stepped into the corridor. He immediately scooped her up in his arms.

Thomas Collier, Lewis presumed. His shirt and slacks were wrinkled, and he had the shadowed cheeks of a man who'd been up for hours. "You made it!" He flashed a grin in Susan's direction. "Linus said he was having trouble finding you."

"I didn't hear the phone," Susan said. "I was out shopping."

"With a friend," Linus added.

"So I see." Thomas turned his attention to Lewis. "Hello."

"Congratulations," Lewis replied. There was no welcoming handshake as the man had his hands full with his daughter, but part of Lewis wondered if there would have been one anyway. Clearly, Thomas was the more serious of the two. His gaze, laser-like in its focus, had a hint of wariness.

"Thank you," he replied. "Kid was an impatient little guy—Rosie barely got settled before he decided to appear. Fifteen minutes later and he might have popped out in the lift." The second half was directed at Linus and Susan.

"Sounds like a Collier," Linus said. "Susan was born in the back seat."

"Only because Belinda thought a back seat delivery would make for better drama," Susan replied. Her face was beet red, the poor thing.

Not knowing what else to do, Lewis wrapped an arm around her waist. "If you're going to make an entrance, might as well make it memorable, right, luv?" He pecked her on the cheek.

Out of the corner of his eye, he saw both Collier brothers raised their eyebrows.

"Daddy, can I see Mummy now?" Maddie asked.

"Sure, sweetheart. Everyone can."

One by one, the family stepped inside the pastel-colored room where a beautiful and tired-looking brunette lay in bed. A few feet away, in a clear plastic bassinet, a tiny bundle lay swaddled in a soft yellow blanket.

"Noel Christopher Collier." Pride filled Thomas's whisper.

"He looks like Dad," Linus said. "Only with a little more hair."

"You're a jerk," Susan said. "He's beautiful. Really, really beautiful."

"All Rosalind's doing. She's the one who did the work." The adoration in Thomas's voice was palpable.

Lewis stood by the door and watched the scene evolve. So much love and pride in one small room. Susan had told him on the way over that the Collier legacy meant everything to her older brother. It was evident. You could feel the sense of family in the air. How could Susan not see it? That she was part of the circle.

He wasn't. He was the outsider. The unexpected, unwanted guest being politely tolerated.

His eyes sought Susan. She was frowning

at him from across the bassinet. "Why are you standing by the door?" she asked.

"Coffee. Thought I'd pop down and get us some." It was the first excuse that came to mind. He needed space to clear his head. A cafeteria run fit the bill.

Coward that he was, he slipped out the door without waiting for her reply.

"Hold on! I'll go with you." Linus's voice called out.

Great. Instead of an escape, he was going to get an escort. The sandy-haired man caught up with him just as the elevator door opened.

"I figured you might need some help carrying everything," he said with a grin. "Both Maddie and Rosalind put in an order for milk and cookies. We might as well buy a half dozen. Susan never met a cookie she didn't like either."

Something about the joke grated on his nerves. "So what? Lots of people like cookies."

"True, but Susan's love of cookies is legendary. We've been teasing her about it since we were kids."

"I'm sure she loved that," Lewis muttered. Already self-conscious because she didn't look like her mother or brothers, her being teased about her eating habits must have stung. Now he understood why she thought she didn't fit in.

"Did you say something?" Linus asked.

"Talking to myself," Lewis replied. Wasn't his place to pick a fight with Susan's brother.

Linus however, wasn't ready to let it go. He moved so he was in front of Lewis, his back to the elevator buttons. Arms folded across his chest, he gave Lewis another long, studious look. "You're annoyed, aren't you?"

"No," Lewis lied. "Just don't think you should be singling her out when everyone has a sweet tooth."

"Huh," Linus said.

"What's that supposed to mean?"

"Nothing," the man replied. "It's nice to know you're protective of Susan's feelings."

Lewis felt his shoulders tightening. "Shouldn't I be? Seems to me, a lot of people should care about Susan's feelings."

"Perhaps, but not all of them are known to go through women like water."

"No. Some of them are related."

Linus's eyebrows shot up and for a second, Lewis worried he'd pushed his luck too far. Then he saw what looked like a gleam of respect.

"Are we going to see you at the gathering

at Christmas?" her brother asked, changing the topic.

"Your company party? Absolutely. I promised Susan I'd be there with bells on."

"No, I meant the wedding on Christmas Eve. Well, vow renewal, second wedding. Whatever you want to call it."

Lewis thought back to the day they'd signed their agreement and the way Susan had hedged when he mentioned the holidays. She clearly didn't want him at a family event.

"The holidays haven't really come up yet," he replied. "We're taking things one day at a time."

"Oh," Linus said. Awkwardness filled the small space. "Well, perhaps we'll see you there," he replied.

"Maybe." Probably not. Weddings were for family, not fake boyfriends.

Why the thought made his stomach hurt, he didn't know.

"Your friend Lewis seems much more low-key than I expected," Thomas remarked shortly after Linus and Lewis left the room. Susan had hoped new fatherhood would distract him, but no such luck.

"What did you expect?" she asked. "That

he'd show up…" She was about to say shirt-less and carrying a bottle of Cristal, but a quick look at Maddie reminded her that wasn't appropriate. "…ready to go crazy? I told you, he's not that person anymore."

"Relax. I wasn't trying to criticize the guy."

No, only lobbing a passive-aggressive comment in his direction. "Lewis is a lot…more… than people give him credit for," she told him. "He's smart, he's gentle, he's considerate…"

"Handsome."

Her sister-in-law lay in bed, her eyes half-closed, with Maddie curled up by her side. Exhausted from the excitement, the little girl was nearly asleep but Rosalind had clearly been listening.

Rosalind stroked her daughter's hair. "He's very handsome," she repeated. "The tabloids don't do him justice."

"No, they don't," Susan agreed. There were times when she would look at him quickly and the sheer perfection of his profile made her breath catch.

"I still can't believe my sister is going out with Champagne Lewis," Thomas said.

"Why?" Because she wasn't a supermodel? Because she was a pathetic shrew? "Is it really such a big stretch?"

"You've got to admit, you two are different."

"Not as much as you'd think," she replied. Maybe on the outside, but on this inside they were two odd peas in a pod. The thought made her smile. "Anyway, it doesn't matter. We're not…"

Her brother, who'd been staring at his new-born son, turned his head. "Not what?"

"Running off and getting married anytime soon."

She almost said they weren't really dating. But it was a secret and if she told Thomas the truth, he'd use it to justify thinking Lewis was still some kind of "bad boy." Which he wasn't. He was everything she said and more.

And she was going to hold on to the illusion for as long as she could.

"For goodness' sake, stop interrogating the woman," Rosalind said in a sleepy voice. "Her love life is none of our business. We don't need to butt in."

"If you remember, she had no problem butting into ours," Thomas said.

Susan winced. She *knew* he still held a grudge over her interference last winter.

"That was different," Rosalind said. "We had our collective heads in the clouds. We wouldn't have had Noel if she hadn't said anything. Now be quiet so I can get some sleep."

"Thank you," Susan replied. Her brother looked down at his feet.

"You're welcome," Rosalind said. "Besides, we already know he's special or you wouldn't have brought him to the hospital."

We already know he's special or you wouldn't have brought him to the hospital.

Her sister-in-law's words stuck in Susan's head the entire way home.

When Lewis and Linus had returned from the cafeteria, she noticed a distinct change in her faux boyfriend's manner. He seemed distant.

"Thank you for coming to the hospital with me," she said. "I know it wasn't quite the fun day you had planned."

"You're welcome. I just hope I wasn't in the way."

"Hardly. I was more worried my brothers would pin you down and interrogate you. They didn't, did they?"

"No."

"Linus didn't say anything stupid when the two of you went to get coffee?"

"No."

The distance was driving her insane. Reaching across the seat, she brushed her fingers across the back of his hand. "What's wrong?"

"Nothing. Seriously," he added as though sensing she was about to press. "It... I'm not used to being included in family events is all."

And he felt out of place. The pieces suddenly came together. "I'm glad you were there," she told him.

"Were you?"

"Yes. Very much. I'm glad my brothers got to see firsthand how good a man you are."

"Now you're reaching." He gave a soft laugh.

"All right, maybe a little. But I think Linus will come around. Thomas...he might be a harder sell. He has a highly overdeveloped sense of responsibility. I used to tell him he had *monomania*, which is a fancy way of saying he's hyperfocused on the business. Comes from listening to our grandfather drone on about the family legacy during his formative years."

"You're playing armchair psychologist again."

"Force of habit." Understanding what made people tick made dealing with them easier. If she could link a reason to an action, then it took away some of the sting. Sometimes, anyway. "Plus, I've spent a lot of time observing my brothers."

"Are you sure you studied the whole picture?" he asked.

"After more than two and a half decades, I'd better have. What makes you ask?"

He shrugged. "No reason. Just that I didn't get the impression either man was acting out of responsibility. Doesn't really matter, though, does it? What they think? After all…"

After all, it wasn't as though he would be a long-term part of her life.

"I'm curious," Lewis said suddenly. Turning sideways, he rested an elbow against the back of the seat. Grateful to have him in her orbit, Susan shifted as well so that they sat face-to-face, their knees touching. "What would your psychology books say about me?"

"You want me to psychoanalyze you?"

"Haven't you already?"

"Maybe." She looked at her lap. "I might have kicked around a few concepts." They only served to depress her.

"Like what?" he asked.

"Why do you care?"

"Color me curious. You sound so certain about your brothers. Makes me curious what you think of me."

Was it really curiosity or was he trying to send her a message? Reminding her not to get too attached.

"What if I don't want to share?"

"Then I'll presume the worst." Lewis's grin was overly wide. "And I'll pester you until you give up the info."

"Fine." He *would* pester her too. "Keep in mind this is completely nonscientific, but if I had to make a hypothesis, I would say children who grew up in foster homes are prone to anxiety, commitment issues, low self-esteem and often have a resulting fear of abandonment."

Lewis didn't answer and the shadows made it impossible to read his expression completely. Susan's stomach sank. "It's only a theory," she said, turning to face the front once more.

"Low self-esteem? Seriously?" she heard him say. "Do I seem like I have low self-esteem to you?"

"I wouldn't say low," Susan replied. Although, he *had* been worried about being accepted at the fund-raiser.

"No offense, luv, but I think you might want to rethink your theory. Excepting for the other night—which was an extraordinary circumstance—my self-esteem and anxiety are just fine."

"And fear of commitment? Am I wrong about that one?" She probably shouldn't ask with the driver present, but she couldn't help herself.

"Depends. Is fear the same as disinterest?"

"No." Fear was better. Fear implied there might be a chance.

"Good to know," he said, nodding.

So much for an answer. On the other hand, did she really need one? The warning was clear. There was a warning hidden in his question—*don't get too attached or think long-term*.

Fine. Then she would take what she could for as long as she could get it.

They moved on to other topics. Thanks to Noel's arrival, they never finished their Christmas shopping and now Susan had to buy a baby gift in addition to the other items on her list.

"Why don't we go tomorrow?" Lewis said, for the driver's benefit, Susan suspected. "I know a great restaurant in Soho. We can grab brunch and then hit Regent Street again. What do you think?"

"Sure." She noticed he was pulling out his wallet to pay. Did that mean he intended to stay? Her heart skipped a beat.

"So, what's the plan?" she asked once they'd stepped outside. The car's taillights disappeared into the traffic.

"Tonight? We grab some takeout, watch a movie and I sleep on your sofa."

A right proper sleepover. All aboveboard and completely phony. But she was tired of phony. She was a woman, dammit. She wanted to be held and kissed like a woman.

The moonless night left his face bathed in shadows, making it impossible to read his expression. His eyes appeared dark and hooded. The warmth from his body floated around her, enveloping her with his scent. One she couldn't label and that was uniquely him.

Take what you can, a voice whispered in her ear.

"You…you don't have to sleep on the sofa."

Lewis stepped back. "I'm not sure that's a good idea."

"Oh." Rejection cut through her. Hugging her midsection, she struggled to keep the disappointment from her voice.

"It's not that I wouldn't want to sleep with you," he said. "In fact…"

"Don't," Susan said. She so didn't want to have this conversation. "The last thing I need to hear is a lot of phony flattery and excuses. You made it very clear that you weren't interested in me in that way. It was stupid of me to think you might change your mind."

Beyond stupid. She wanted to go inside, pull the covers over her head and pretend the last five minutes had never happened.

"Susan…"

"It's been a really long day, Lewis," she said, cutting him off again. "Why don't we say good-night. We can wake up superearly and pretend we spent the night together, okay?"

"Susan…"

"Good night, Lewis. I'm sorry you have to…"

He kissed her.

He closed the distance between them and he kissed her. Like an animal springing on its prey, his mouth covered Susan's before she could make a sound. Her eyes fluttered shut as she melted into him. Wow, could this man kiss. This wasn't gentle or sweet like the other kisses though. This kiss was primal. The kind of kiss that claimed a person. Clutching his shoulders, Susan met him need for need until neither of them could breathe. They broke apart, their breaths loud and ragged in the night air.

"Still think I don't want to sleep with you?" Lewis asked between gasps.

If he didn't, he was a damn good liar. Her body, from head to toe, believed him. "Then why?" Why did she feel like he was still about to reject her?

Lewis's hands were tangled in her curls, combing them away from her face over and over. "A woman like you is made for serious relationships," he said. "The kind a man dates when he's thinking about things like homes and kids. If I…" He smiled. "If I were the kind of guy who thought of such things, I'd tether you to my side for eternity."

"But…?" Susan asked. There was definitely a but coming whether she wanted to hear it or not.

Lewis's hand slid from her hair to cup her cheek momentarily. "But I'm not that kind of guy."

"I know." He'd made his views on commitment quite clear in the taxi.

Take what you can, the voice reminded.

"What if I said I didn't care?" she asked.
"What if I'm okay with here and now?"

She reached down and entwined her fingers with his. "Houses and kids are nice dreams, but sometimes a woman just wants to feel wanted."

Her heart was in her throat when she finished. Talk about laying it all on the table. It was up to Lewis now. If he rejected her, so be it. At least she'd know.

Lewis's hand was cupping her cheek again. The whites of his eyes were brilliant in the dark as he searched her face. "Are you sure?"

Could he not see the certainty on her face? Releasing his hand, Susan slid her palms upward along the padded front of his jacket until she reached the point where the zipper stopped. He was layers of darkness. Navy jacket, black sweater. With a deep breath to steel her nerves, she slipped her gloved hand under his jacket. "What do you think?" she asked.

What felt like the longest beat of her life passed. Susan kept her eyes locked with his; the knot of nerves in her chest twisted.

There was the rustle of nylon and suddenly, Lewis's hands were at the front of her wool coat. One by one, he undid the buttons, his eyes never leaving hers, until her coat hung open.

"I think," he said, playing with the hem of her sweater, "that we should go inside."

"This is new," Lewis said later, wrapped together with her in a cocoon of blankets, in Susan's king-size bed. Her cheek was resting over his heart and the taste of her kisses was still on his lips.

"What's new?"

"Staying awake." He buried his nose in her curls, inhaling the vanilla scent of her shampoo. "Usually I fall asleep." Or start planning his escape. Pulling a woman close to savor in the afterglow wasn't his style.

And yet, here he was, with Susan curled against his body, drawing lazy circles on his torso.

"You romantic devil."

"Never said I wasn't a player, luv."

For some reason he was determined to hammer that shameful point home tonight. He immediately regretted the statement when Susan's hand stilled. There was no reason to be harsh. She knew this was a temporary arrangement.

"Did you know that you're the first woman I've slept with stone-cold sober?"

"Seriously?" She lifted her head. Even in the dark, he could see her surprise. "You mean you haven't…?"

"Nope. Been too busy keeping my head down, proving I'm a good boy."

"Oh, you were good…"

"I know," he replied. Her laugh vibrated through him, and he pulled her close. Could you feel someone rolling their eyes? "You weren't so bad yourself, you know."

"Glad I didn't disappoint."

"Definitely not." Being with her was…well, it was amazing. He'd mapped every inch of her soft curves with his hands, and then went back and did the same with his mouth. Something else he'd never felt the need to do: savor the experience.

All this newness made him uneasy. Different was turning out to be unnerving.

"You didn't tell me your brother and his wife were renewing their wedding vows."

Her hand stilled again.

"Linus told me. He seemed surprised I wasn't attending."

"I didn't think you'd want to go," she replied. "You can, of course. If you want."

Gee, with that kind of enthusiasm… "Don't worry about it. I only mentioned it so you wouldn't be caught off guard if Linus mentions we talked about it."

Honestly, he didn't know why he'd brought it up. Maybe he was looking for further affirmation that she wasn't looking for more.

Or was he hoping for the opposite?

Listen to him. One night with the woman and he was psychoanalyzing too. It was a short-term arrangement. No need to turn the affair into anything deeper. Once they holidays ended, he and Susan would go their separate ways.

And he was fine with that.

Really.

Truly.

Wasn't he?

CHAPTER EIGHT

"I WANT TO TELL you a story. Once upon a time there was a boy who really, really loved sports. Every chance he got, he practiced. Good weather. Bad weather. He worked at becoming the best he could be. And you know what? It paid off. He became a superstar.

"But then you know what happened? He stopped working so hard. He started taking his skills for granted. He developed bad habits. He told himself, 'I'm a superstar. I don't need to practice that much.' For a while, he got away with it. Eventually though, his athletic skill started to slip. Suddenly, he wasn't the superstar anymore. He was just a guy with a lot of bad habits who'd forgotten what was really important."

Susan sat in a far row of the indoor facility listening to Lewis tell the youth ambassadors his story. He'd told her last night that he wanted to use the opportunity to teach the kids what happened when they lost sight of what mattered. It was impressive, how honest Lewis was being about his own failings. Heartbreaking too, when you realized how much his partying had cost him. Thank goodness he'd seen the light before the lifestyle killed him.

Otherwise, the world would be a bleaker place. Not to mention her bed. She smiled recalling the last few nights. Since the night Noel was born, the two of them had been engaged in a full-fledged affair, and it was better than she could have imagined. The way Lewis touched her when they made love made her feel like the most beautiful woman in the world. It was going to be awfully hard going back to life without him after their fake love affair was over.

Something inside her cracked a little at the thought. They'd attend a few more events, the company party and then say goodbye. Unless, that is, they needed to continue the arrangement a little while longer.

How sad was that? Hoping Lewis's image didn't improve enough so she could keep him in her life a few weeks longer.

"He's doing a marvelous job. Goes to show

people love a good redemption story. Even kids."

A man she didn't recognize sat down in the seat next to her.

"Michael Ryder," he said.

So this was the infamous Michael, Lewis's agent. He looked like a talent agent. His pin-striped suit was very expensive and his hair very styled. He also obviously had a penchant for cigars. The scent clung to his clothes. Trying not to wrinkle her nose, Susan shifted herself a little farther away.

"I have to admit," he said after they'd shaken hands, "that when Lewis first came up with this crazy scheme, I had my doubts. But it looks like it might have some value after all. He never would have scored an event like this without you."

On the field, the kids broke out in laughter over something Lewis had said. "He doesn't need me to help him secure speaking engagements," Susan replied. "He's perfectly capable of charming people on his own."

Ryder smirked. "Spoken like a true loyal girlfriend."

"Don't have to be a girlfriend to recognize his abilities."

"Wow. You're good. I can see why Lewis was so keen on partnering up with you."

"Is there something I can do for you, Mr. Ryder?" Susan decided she didn't like the man. He was too keen on reminding her she wasn't Lewis's real girlfriend.

"I came by to tell you that *Personal Magazine* is interested in doing a story about the two of you. A reporter's going to sit down with you both next week."

"Great. Lewis will be thrilled."

"Yeah. They loved the whole love as the redeemer angle. They're bringing a photographer to get some shots of you both at Lewis's apartment. Readers love that homey behind-the-scenes stuff. You *have* been to his apartment, haven't you?" he asked in a low voice.

"Yes." Just the past night, as a matter of fact. Although his tone was so annoying she wouldn't have admitted if the answer was no.

"Good. Make sure you know where all the glassware and stuff is. We want to ensure you look at home. Know what I mean?"

"Why don't I leave some intimates on the bathroom floor to really hammer home the message?"

"Funny. Stick to leaving an extra toothbrush."

"Fine. I'll make sure to buy one tonight." She seriously did not like this man. "Unless there's something else you need to discuss, I'd like to continue watching Lewis."

Unfortunately though, it looked like she'd missed the end of his talk. The kids were breaking into groups for some kind of skills training. While the volunteers played shepherd, Lewis walked to a nearby bench and stripped off his sweatshirt. Susan's eyes automatically sought out the strip of skin on his back that came exposed when his shirt pulled up. He had the most beautiful back. She loved watching the muscles play across his shoulders when he moved his arms. She loved running her hands over those shoulders too.

"Oh, man, you've got it bad."

Hadn't the agent moved on? Susan slid her gaze sideways. "I beg your pardon?" she asked.

"The look on your face. You look like you're worshipping the guy." Susan rolled her eyes. "Don't get me wrong," Ryder said. "If you look at him like that during the interview, there won't be a person alive who won't believe you're not madly in love. Problem will be getting him to look at you the same way.

The Lewis I know has trouble remembering girls' names."

So did the Lewis she knew. "That was when he was drinking," Susan said. "He's not the same person now."

"Only, I'm not sure sobriety translates into acting skills. If he were really a one-woman man we wouldn't be doing this crap."

The man made a very good, albeit harsh, point. One that settled hard in the pit of her stomach.

"You needn't worry. Lewis knows how to put on a show when he has to."

"Good." The agent started to stand, only to sit back down. "Hey, do yourself a favor, will you? Don't get too sucked in by our boy."

"Don't worry," Susan replied. "I'm not stupid. I know exactly where I stand with Lewis."

Besides, his warning was too little, too late. She was already irreparably sucked in.

When Lewis was a kid and played his first game in net, he had been on top of the world. Sure, it was only a street game, but he remembered how it had felt like he'd won the World Cup. He'd succeeded and the neighborhood kids liked him. Over the years, he'd had many moments of victory, but as amazing as they were, none had the pureness of that first game.

Until today.

He lay prone on the turf, the smell of rubber backing tickling his nose. "That's it," he said. "I'm done."

Thirty-six kids faced off with him. Thirty-six kids beat him and scored. Lewis had to work harder than he'd ever worked to make sure each ball just missed his outstretched hands. By the tenth or eleventh goal, the kids knew he was letting them win, but they didn't care. If the laughter was any indication, they were having too much fun. So was Lewis.

Pushing himself to his knees, he blew the whistle around his neck. "All right. Fun as it's been, we've got to pack it up." A loud moan filled the facility, pumping him even higher. "What's with the booing? You're going to a Christmas party! With cake."

That got them moving to the sidelines quickly.

A girl, who looked to be around nine years old, approached him. "Mr. Matolo? Can I take a selfie with you?"

"Sure. Give it over and we'll take a proper

one," he said. How much things had changed. When he was nine, he barely knew what a cell phone was let alone had one stashed in his equipment bag. And when he was playing, he'd been too arrogant to give fans the proper time.

He stayed on his knees so the two of them would be the same height. Of course, as soon as the others saw what was happening, more came running over with their phones to do the same. Not all though. Several of the kids looked over and went back to their bags. Lewis noticed a couple pulling out scraps of paper including one who tore off part of his lunch bag. Some things hadn't changed after all. There were still kids going without.

An idea came to him. Cupping his hands into a megaphone, he called into the stands. "Hey, Susie! Come here for a moment, and bring your phone." He smiled as she got up and started toward the stairs. Susan didn't know it, but she'd been his good luck charm. Knowing she was in the stands, believing in him, gave him the courage to tell his story. He loved the way she believed in him. Every time he looked in her direction, an empowering warmth spread through his insides. Different from the heat of attraction, it made him want to prove her trust wasn't misplaced.

"Mr. Matolo? Can I have your autograph?" It was the kid with the torn lunch bag bringing him back to the moment at hand.

"Hold on for one minute," Lewis told him. "I need to make a quick announcement."

He cupped his hands once again. "If anyone wants to take a picture, but doesn't have a camera, come get in line. My friend will take the pictures and have Mr. Redmayne send you a copy." Surely the director wouldn't mind doing a little extra to make sure the kids were happy.

While waiting for Susan, he signed paper scraps and several of the kids' T-shirts. He was in the middle of writing on one kid's shoulder when he noticed a shadow fall across the crowd.

"I owe you an apology," Graham Montclark said. "I came by because Chris was a nervous wreck over hiring you. You never mentioned you were a motivational speaker when you made your offer the other night."

"I'm not," Lewis replied. "I simply told these kids the truth. If it stops one of them from making the same mistakes I made, all the better."

The other man digested his words. Lewis hoped they'd come out as sincerely as intended. A word from Graham Montclark would be the in he needed.

"Do you have any idea how many stairs there are between the stands and this playing field?" A slightly out-of-breath Susan came walking toward them. From her adorably flushed cheeks, he guessed she'd run the entire way. "Not to mention security guards. I almost had to cheat on you in order to gain access. Hello, Mr. Montclark. Nice to see you again."

"It's good to see you as well, Ms. Collier. I was just telling Lewis here that he should consider a career as a motivational speaker."

"He was inspiring, wasn't he?" The way she beamed in his direction made Lewis's insides turn end over end.

"While I appreciate the compliments, all I did was give the kids some straight talk and attention. Nothing special about that."

"Don't sell yourself short," Susan replied. "Perhaps you should consider doing events on the side."

"On the side of what?" Montclark asked. "You're retired aren't you?"

Bless her. Once again, she'd opened the

door for him. When they got home, he was going to kiss every ivory inch of her. "My agent has been talking with a few outlets about my being involved with the media side of the sport. In fact, I think one of the stations might be yours."

"Is that so?" Montclark replied. "I hope they're treating you right."

They weren't treating him at all. "They're being fair." To his surprise, he found he meant it. "After all, as you know, I come with some past baggage."

"I don't usually get involved in day-to-day operations myself, but if anyone gives you trouble, let me know. You've more than impressed me today."

"Thank you. I appreciate the vote of confidence." His eyes caught Susan's. Unbelievable. Was it possible this whole crazy plan was actually going to work? Was he actually going to rebuild his reputation and return to the spotlight? If so, it was all because of the woman he'd picked for a partner. She really was his good luck charm.

His stomach immediately sank. What was he going to do when their arrangement ended?

Nothing. He didn't know why he kept asking himself the question.

"Mr. Matolo, will you take our pictures now?" one of the children asked.

"Absolutely! We've wasted enough time." He turned his attention back to the task at hand. "Miss Susan, snap away. We've got a Christmas party to attend."

He could dwell on end dates another time.

Susan had to hand it to her brother. He didn't do things halfway. Thus it was no surprise when she walked into the annual Collier's holiday party to discover Christmas had arrived early. The ballroom was a winter wonderland of crystal and white like the ice castle in Maddie's favorite animated film. In fact, there was an ice castle. A giant sculpture in the middle of the room, around which were tables laden with hors d'oeuvres. Behind her, outside the ballroom, there was a staircase decked with white poinsettias. She hadn't gone upstairs yet, but she'd been told it led to a rooftop bar where people could sit around a fire pit and sip hot chocolate.

It was magnificent, and she was standing in the doorway alone.

Only for a moment. "Who takes home the castle?" Linus asked, joining her. Susan breathed a sigh of relief. As substitute host and hostess, she and Linus were expected to arrive early in order to greet all the guests. After his flakeout over Maria's wedding, she'd been worried he'd leave her to the wolves again. She looked him up and down. "You made it," she said.

"Thomas would have killed me if I hadn't, same as you," he replied. "I wasn't in the mood to court death this holiday."

"Good call." If Thomas hadn't killed him, she would have. "Let's hope next year he doesn't decide to have another baby so we can hand the job back to him."

"Sounds good to me." He looked around the room, then back to her. "Where's your boyfriend?"

"He had some business to take care of." That was exactly how Lewis put it too. Business to take care of. "He'll be here soon," she replied.

Her answer came out more defensively than she meant. Of course he would be there. He'd promised.

She adjusted the neckline of her dress again. The red-and-silver brocade was flashier than her usual style. Knee-length and classically draped in the front, it had a plunging back. The minute she saw it, visions of Lewis kissing her exposed back danced in her head. She couldn't wait for him to see her in it.

At the current moment, she'd settle for just seeing him come through the door. "Where's your date?" she asked Linus. "Or are you going solo again this year?"

Her brother shoved his hands in his pockets. "What do you think?" he asked.

Single then. If Lewis didn't show, then she'd at least have a dance partner.

Honestly, why was she worrying about Lewis? He'd promised. Maybe it was because the holidays were drawing closer. After this, Lewis had no obligations to her. She thought after Graham Montclark's comment the other day that he might discuss their future, and whether he thought they should continue their faux romance past New Year's. Instead, he'd said nothing. When they were together, it was easy to pretend they didn't have an arrangement; other times Susan felt like she was in a holding pattern. One ruled by nights of incredible wonder.

"You're making that face again," Linus said.

Susan frowned. "What face?"

"The one you've been making all week. Where your eyes glaze over and you get this dreamy smile. Somebody's in love." He nudged her with his shoulder.

"Stop being an ass," Susan replied as her cheeks warmed. "I'm not in love."

"Could have fooled me. Little Miss Dreamy Eyes."

Oh, brother. Please don't tell her she was going to be stuck listening to his stupid nicknames. Linus loved his stupid nicknames. "Lewis and I are enjoying each other's company, that is all," she told him.

"Uh-huh."

"We are. I'm not in love with Lewis Matolo."

Aren't you? After days of being ignored, the question slammed into her brain. How long was she going to pretend the man hadn't gotten under skin?

Easy, she answered back. For as long as it took. Fake it till you make it, as the saying went.

Since she was having the conversation in her head, however, Linus felt comfortable continuing. "He certainly seems to care about you. Nearly took my head off in the hospital elevator the day Noel was born."

"What? What did you do?" Besides mentioning the wedding. She *knew* something had happened that afternoon.

"Why are you assuming I did anything?"

"Because I've known you since birth," Susan told him. "You always do something."

Linus was insistent. "I swear I did nothing. At least not on purpose. All I said was that we needed to buy extra cookies because you love them so much. He suggested I stop picking on you."

Warmth seeped through her veins. She couldn't remember the last time someone had defended her honor.

"I'm not surprised. Lewis likes to look out for the underdog," she told her brother.

Linus gave her a look. "You're an underdog?"

"He was defending me against a comment you made. What do you think?"

"Either way, he's not what I expected," Linus said.

"I told you but you and Thomas refused to believe me. Thomas still doesn't believe me."

"Meh." Linus waved off her complaint. "You know Thomas. Anything that could remotely impact the company gets him uptight."

Susan looked away. He would really hate if he knew the truth then.

"If it will make you feel better, I'll talk

to him," Linus said. "Let him know Lewis passes my sniff test."

"Thank you. I'd appreciate that. And for the record… I hate when you make jokes about my sweet tooth."

Linus leaned back in surprise. "We've been making those jokes since we were kids."

"I know. Thanks to my mother." Belinda used to love to point out how calories weren't Susan's friend and never missed an opportunity to remind her with a subtle jab. "Might as well just say you think I'm fat."

"We don't think that." Linus continued to look shocked. "We just know you like cookies."

"Well, it feels like you think so. Especially since that's how Belinda meant it."

"Belinda was a piece of work. None of us should take anything she said seriously."

Easy for him to say; Linus and Thomas weren't her children. "Still, I would appreciate if you stopped making the joke. Especially around my… Lewis."

"No need to worry there," Linus said. "He didn't find the comment funny either. In fact, he pretty much said the same thing as you did. About you feeling like we were calling you fat."

Because Lewis understood her. Susan couldn't help her smile or the fullness in her heart. She'd always wondered what it would be like, having someone in her life who knew what she was thinking or feeling without her having to say a word. To be able to look across a crowd and know she wasn't alone.

"You're getting that dreamy look again," Linus said. "You really like this guy, don't you?"

"Yeah, I do." More than liked, to be honest.

"I can tell. How come you didn't invite him to Thomas's vow renewal then?"

The question caught her by surprise. "Because it's a family thing."

"Doesn't mean you can't include your boyfriend. You brought him to the hospital."

"That was different. He was with me when you called. The ceremony on Christmas Eve is going to be intimate."

"And gathered 'round Rosalind's hospital bed eating cookies and letting Maddie climb on him wasn't?" He frowned. "You're afraid we're going to give him a hard time, aren't you?"

"Wouldn't you?"

"Absolutely, but in the best-natured way

possible. That's what big brothers do. Tell you what," he said. "If you're worried, the five of us can go out beforehand and bond with him properly."

Oh, yeah, she could see Lewis jumping at the opportunity to have a "bonding" dinner with the Collier clan. She could picture the scene now. The three of them eating curry and peppering Lewis with questions. Her temporary relationship was going to be short enough; she didn't need their curiosity ending the arrangement prematurely.

"That isn't necessary," she told him.

"Sure it is. You said yourself, we weren't being fair to him. This will be our way of letting him know we approve of his dating our sister and we welcome him to the family."

"Really, you don't have to," Susan said.

"Why are you fighting the idea. You just asked me to be nice. If the guy's going to be around for a while…"

"He's not."

Her brother's eyes narrowed. "What are you talking about? Don't tell me you two are on the outs already? Is that why he's not here tonight?"

"No, no. I told you, Lewis will be here."

"Then what gives? Why so certain you two

will be done? You've got to have a little more faith than that, Susie."

"Maybe I would if I didn't have an exit date."

"I beg your pardon."

Susan sighed. If she'd known they were going to start suggesting family get-togethers, she would have told them the truth from the start. But since when did her brothers bond with anyone? Let alone someone connected with her? "We aren't really dating." Briefly she explained their arrangement.

"You're kidding," Linus said when she was finished. Susan was stunned by his stunned expression. Maybe she and Lewis had done a better job pretending than she thought. "Why would you do something like that?"

"I told you, Lewis needs…"

"I mean you. Champagne Lewis I get, but why would you get involved in something like this?"

She shrugged. "Maybe I wanted an image makeover too."

"Unbelievable. Thomas is going to have a cow, you know."

A big mad cow too, which was why she kept silent in the first place. But only if Thomas found out. Which didn't have to happen. "Then don't tell him," she said. "The whole affair will be over before Thomas gets back from paternity leave. There's no reason for him to get involved."

"Except for the whole Collier's thing. You know how he is about the company reputation."

"All the more reason to not spoil his time with the new baby. There's no need to trigger him unnecessarily."

"True." Her brother let out a long, frustrated breath, a sign he was seriously considering the suggestion. "We'll have to talk about this later," he said. "People are starting to arrive."

And the last thing they needed was someone to overhear. "I'm going to go check my hair," she said. "The bun feels loose."

"I'm going to go make sure everything is in order, or whatever it is Thomas expects us to do." He headed toward the back of the room where the event coordinators were congregated.

"Oh, hey," he said, stopping and speaking over his shoulder. "About that other thing we were talking about. You know, the cookies?"

"Yeah?" The abrupt change of topic would

throw her except it was Linus, and Linus was known for it.

"You're nowhere near being fat."

"I know," Susan replied. She was normal. And even if she wasn't, Lewis loved her body. Every porcelain inch, he said. That was all that mattered.

Smiling to herself, she turned and headed to the powder room. On the way, a flash of black caught her eye. It was Courtney minus her partner in crime. Ever since Susan had told them off at work, she and Ginger had limited their interaction to only the most necessary business. Tonight, the woman smirked like a cat as Susan passed her.

Susan was surprised to discover she didn't care.

Imagine that. All this fuss about paying them back tonight, and it no longer seemed to matter.

CHAPTER NINE

FOR THE NEXT forty-five minutes, Susan smiled and said hello to every person who stepped off the elevator. Most responded politely and kept going, way more interested in the free drinks and food than in talking with her. Thankfully. It wasn't until Maria and Hank arrived that she had to make any kind of real conversation.

"Welcome home," she greeted the newlyweds with a smile. "How was America?"

"Big. We had a marvelous time. Especially in Hawaii," Maria answered. "I hated to come back. Don't worry, though, I'll be in the office on Monday. I know you're eager to discuss a few things."

"Maria, honey, it's a Christmas party," Hank said, his voice gently admonishing. "There'll be plenty of time to talk work next week."

His bride blushed. They were still in the phase where bickering in public required restraint. "I know, but this is Susan. I'm sure she wants to bring me up to speed."

Did she do that? Did she spend time at parties working? Susan thought back to different functions. Damn. "Not tonight," she quickly replied. "It's Christmas. I don't know about you, but I have more important things to talk about."

"So we read." Maria's remark had all three of them turning a subtle pink.

"Where is Lewis?" Hank asked. "I was hoping to catch up with him. We didn't get to talk very long at the wedding."

Indeed, where was Lewis? Nearly an hour into the party and he still hadn't arrived.

"He…um…got tied up with business and is running late," she repeated for the umpteenth time. "I'm sure he'll be here any minute."

"See? I'm not the only one distracted by business," Maria said.

"Apparently not." But as Hank answered, he flashed a sympathetic look in Susan's direction. It was the look of someone who knew Lewis's past habits. He's not the same man, Susan wanted to holler. A hard sell seeing how it was at their wedding that Lewis had a pair of drinks tossed in his face.

Just then the elevator dinged. The doors slid open and there was Lewis looking like he'd stepped off a runway in a black velvet blazer. Susan's heart leaped to her throat at the sight of him.

So much for faking not being in love. It'd be easier pretending Lewis wasn't gorgeous or Collier's sold auto parts.

She broadened her smile. Her feelings— or rather, their repercussions—were an issue for another time.

"I am so sorry I'm late, luv. My meeting went far longer than I thought." The apology tumbled from Lewis's mouth as he slipped an arm around her waist. "You look delicious," he added, kissing her cheek. "Maybe it was a good thing I wasn't there when you were getting ready or we'd both be late."

"If you're trying to flatter me into forgiving your lateness, it's working," Susan told him.

"Good. I'll flatter you some more later. Welcome back from the honeymoon, you two," he said, turning to Hank and Maria with a smile.

This was one of those times when the relationship felt real. Although they were sleeping together so it was also real in that sense. Deeper was the better word. This was one of those times when the relationship felt deeper. There was a sparkle in his eyes that was easy to mistake as adoration. She needed to remember though, he was just playing a part. Tonight he was honoring his half of the agreement by playing the doting boyfriend.

"I can't believe you two met at our wedding," Maria was saying.

"I told her when you RSVP'd as single, that you wouldn't be going home that way," Hank remarked.

"Which I admit, had me worried. Especially after that thing with Diane and Trish."

Lewis looked up at the ceiling lights. "Diane and Trish! Those were their names! I am really sorry about that little scene. I met those girls during a dark time in my life."

"Well, I'd be more annoyed if I didn't know they're total gold diggers. Hey, I love them," she said to Susan's stunned expression, "but that doesn't mean I don't know what they're like. It's why I agreed to give Lewis your phone number. I figured if he was chasing after you, he wasn't the promiscuous man Hank had made him out to be. Although you should apologize to them," she added, turning to Lewis with a reproachful look.

"I agree," Susan said.

"So do I," Lewis replied. "Which is why I sent them both apology letters explaining everything after the wedding."

"You did?" She smiled at him with pride. "Wait a second," she said. "I thought you just remembered their... You jerk."

Laughing, Lewis pretended to rub the shoulder she'd playfully slapped. "Hey, can't a guy joke around about his bad-boy past? I can't believe you didn't think I would apologize."

"You're right." She was properly chastised. "I should have realized you're too good a man not to own your mistakes."

"Well, I did lead you on, so I can't be too annoyed, can I?" He leaned over and kissed her temple, causing Hank to offer a mock groan.

"Oh, man," his friend said. "You are smitten with a capital *S*. Never thought I'd see the day. Must be a Christmas miracle. Say, the four of us need to go out after the holidays."

Susan tensed. "You mean, in January?" What was it with people suddenly inviting them places?

"Sure. Lewis can help me lie about my glory days before I left academy league."

"Left?" Lewis said. "You were dismissed because your foot couldn't find the ball. You sure you want to ruin whatever lies you told your bride?"

While the three of them laughed, Susan drifted away into thought. January was only a few weeks away. She and Lewis would be done. This marvelous fun-filled night out they were planning would never happen.

"Tuesday?"

Giving a blink, she realized Maria was talking to her. "I know you usually choose to eat at your desk but the wedding proofs will be in so I thought maybe you'd like to join us for once." Maria and several other women went out for lunch every Tuesday.

"Um…maybe," Susan replied.

Maria looked pleased. "Great."

"Hey, babe, I want to grab a drink before the lines at the bar are too long," Hank said. "We'll catch up with the two of you later."

She waited until the couple disappeared into the ballroom before turning to Lewis. "Did I agree to go to lunch and look at wedding photos?"

"Yes, why?"

"No reason. Other than I'm surprised she asked." In the past, when Maria made the offer to join the group for lunch, Susan assumed it was because she'd happened across them as they were headed out.

"Perhaps she's seeing you in a new light," Lewis replied. "Congratulations. Means both of us are getting the makeover we wanted."

"Maybe." Changing the subject, she asked, "How did your business meeting go?"

"I'll tell you all about it later. When we have a chance to talk," he replied.

"We can't talk here?"

"Nah," he said, shaking his head. "This is your night. I'm going to help you make the entire company jealous."

"That was never my goal," Susan said. "Not all of it anyway."

"What was your goal then? Because I seem to remember a woman telling me she wanted to show the whole lot of them."

"I did. I...do. At least that's part of it."

"What do you mean?" The way he looked at her, his expression direct and focused, it felt like he was trying to read her mind. He played with a tendril of hair by her ear. "Is there another reason?"

How did she explain? "I'm not sure I can put it into words," she told him.

"Try."

"All right, but not here." Looking around for a quiet area, she saw that the staircase was empty. It was too early for anyone to venture to the roof. Most of the partygoers were still busy milling about near the bar. "Come with me."

"This is cozy," he said when they stepped outside. "I like the way you think."

"I didn't want anyone listening," she told him. She'd been right about the crowd. The rooftop was empty except for the bartender who was tucked away behind the Plexiglas wall of the bar, out of the cold.

The flames in the gas firepit flickered brightly. Susan led Lewis to one of the sofas making up the surrounding circle.

No sooner had they sat down than the bartender emerged from his shelter, carrying a plaid blanket.

"Welcome to the rooftop," he greeted as he handed the blanket over to Lewis who promptly draped the material around them.

"Wouldn't want you to get cold," he murmured, his breath warm against her temple.

The shiver that followed was anything but cold.

"Can I get you something to drink?" the bartender asked. "The special tonight is peppermint hot chocolate. Guaranteed to warm you from the inside out."

"Depends," Susan mused. "Does it have a holiday name?"

The man looked confused. "Peppermint hot chocolate," he said.

"Then I think we're good," Lewis replied. "We'll create our own warmth." He scooped Susan's legs up over his lap. She gasped as the cold from his hand touched her leg, but then snuggled against his chest. Being in his arms was like being nestled in a wonderfully safe cocoon.

"Now," he said. "Tell me this reason you can't put into words."

For a second, Susan had forgotten what they'd been talking about. "I hate this party," she said, laying her head on his shoulder. "All parties really, but this one most of all. Usually I make up an excuse and stay home, but this year Thomas didn't give me a choice."

"Why do you avoid it?"

"Isn't it obvious?" She was always alone, in a room where she felt like everyone was dreading having to talk with her. "Think of the wedding times ten."

A frown formed on Lewis's face. "It makes you feel like a pathetic loser?"

"Bingo. All these groups of people who know each other chatting away and there I am, with a stupid smile on my face, wondering if any of them will invite me to join them."

"And you were too afraid to join them yourself."

"Not scared." Scared was the wrong word. "More like I could feel the barrier between me and them, if that makes sense. Like I could go over to them, but I would still be the outsider without anything to say. You saw Maria. The only thing she could talk to me about was work." At least it was, before they had Lewis to talk about. "And she's one of the friendliest."

It was embarrassing, listening to herself complain like this. She didn't like revealing this side of herself. For some reason, however, it seemed to happen around Lewis. Whether because the way he looked at her when she spoke loosened her tongue or because she felt he understood, she didn't know.

Losing herself in the blue of the fire, she continued. "Normally, I don't care what they think. We're talking about coworkers and employees. I don't need to be their friend. Every once in a while though...well, that's why I stay home. Being in my apartment is a lot more comfortable than being a wallflower."

"You could simply hang with your family," he said.

"I try, but Thomas believes in mingling and Linus is friends with the entire company. I look like the sad baby sister tagging along." Just like when they were kids.

"So along with getting a little revenge on those bathroom chicks, you wanted me to be here to keep you from feeling alone. Is that what you're telling me?"

"Sort of." The words still weren't completely right. "Have you ever wanted to be that person who everyone noticed? I mean, noticed in a good way? The person the whole room wants to be? Never mind. Forget I asked that." Of course he knew.

"You want to be one of the cool kids," Lewis replied.

"When you put it like that, it sounds so childish." Maybe it was. High school was a long time ago.

She felt Lewis's thumb stroking her dress, right above her hip bone. A slow, steady massage. She focused on the tempo, back and forth, back and forth until the feelings jumbled inside her formed a coherent sentence. "Not cool. Special," she said finally. Lewis went to speak, but she stopped him with a shake of her head. "My brothers, my mother, even my father when he was alive. People pay attention to them. Notice them. People care about what they think because their opinions matter. *They* matter. I want to matter too," she said in a soft voice.

Lewis stared at the woman curled into his side. How could she think she wasn't special? "Oh, luv," he whispered, brushing a wispy tendril from her face.

He knew what she meant. That feeling of being less than the rest of the room. Of waiting to be called out as a fraud and asked to leave. And while Susan was the last person who should feel that way, he knew all the reminding her in the world wouldn't make her believe him. The feeling came from deep inside where words couldn't reach. Only thoughts.

Still, it didn't hurt to tell her. "You don't need me on your arm to matter."

"Don't I though?" She shifted her position, her legs leaving his lap. It added space between them, and he didn't like it. "Do you know how many people have wanted to talk with me at work since we started dating? They look at me differently now. And Courtney and Ginger? They've practically twisted themselves into knots trying to get on my good side. Call me immature," she said, "but I like the attention. That's the reason I wanted you as my date for the party. This might be the one time I get to be the popular girl."

"I'd never call you immature," he told her. She began to pick at the plaid material of the blanket. "If wanting to be popular is a crime, then half the world would be guilty." Including him. Heck, his glass house was probably ten times the size of hers.

"You're wrong though," he told her. "You don't need the spotlight to matter."

Like he expected she would, she scoffed softly. "You can have all the adulation and popularity you want, but all you really need are a few people who care. One person even."

"Easy for you to say."

Was it? There was a lesson for him in those words, but now wasn't the time to pick them apart.

"You sell yourself too short. You matter to your family. I know you don't believe it, but you matter to your brothers. And Maddie…"

She smiled at the mention of her niece. "Maddie's my little angel."

Noel would be one soon enough as well, he suspected. She wasn't the horrible, unlikable shrew she painted herself out to be.

She was amazing really.

If someone had told him a few weeks ago, when they hashed out this arrangement, how much he would enjoy their time together, he wouldn't have believed them. Today wouldn't have happened. He wouldn't have achieved half the success if she hadn't been by his side.

An inexplicable fullness gripped him. Looking at her now, white lights twinkling about her, he'd never seen anything as lovely.

"You matter to me too," he said. The reverence in his voice didn't come close to capturing how he felt. "A lot. You matter to me a lot."

The look in her eye said she didn't believe him.

Very well. He would just have to show her the best way he knew possible. Pulling her close, he kissed her.

And kissed her again.

"Let's get out of here," he murmured against her mouth. There was more he wanted to tell her. Plus he hadn't been kidding about

how delicious she looked. Between her choc-
olate-tinged kisses and her creamy bare back,
she had him starving.

"I can't. I promised Thomas." Her argument would have been more persuasive if
she weren't kissing him back in between sen-
tences. Eventually, she pulled away, out of
his mouth's reach. "Besides, at the very least
I deserve a dance downstairs."

Lewis took a good look at her mussed hair
and swollen lips. There was no hiding what
they'd been up to, that was for sure.

Well, she'd wanted people to notice.

Linus was stepping onto the dais to speak
when they entered the ballroom. As soon as
he saw them, he motioned impatiently for
Susan to join him. Lewis stepped back into
the shadows and watched as she hurried to the
front of the ballroom. At least a half-dozen
heads turned in her direction.

And she thought no one noticed her.

When she reached the stage area, Linus
whispered something in her ear. Judging from
the way she turned crimson, he could guess
the commentary.

"I promise I won't stand up here long,"
Linus said, "because I know you'd much
rather eat and drink free food than listen to

anyone named Collier drone on. But my sister Susan and I wanted to take a few minutes and say thank you. This has been a true comeback year for Collier's. Thanks to your efforts, the Collier name is poised to continue succeeding, not only for the upcoming year, but with luck, for another four hundred!"

When the polite laughter subsided, he raised his glass. "Seriously, Collier's would be nothing without our employees. So on behalf of Thomas, Susan and myself—along with all our executive staff—thank you, happy holidays and a very happy New Year. Now get out there on the dance floor and have a good time!"

The crowd applauded, and the deejay struck up a party song. Lewis waited until Susan stepped off the stage before sauntering toward her.

"Now can we go home?" He already knew the answer, but he wanted to see her skin blush again when he made the suggestion.

At the same time, Linus walked by. "Nice of you to join us," he said, giving them both a look. "We'll talk later, Susan."

Lewis looked back at her with a frown. "Are you in trouble?"

"Nothing dire. Although you could have told me my bun was falling."

"Is it? I hadn't noticed." His hands settled on her hips, fingers splaying outward. "Everything seems in place to me." He paused. "Oh. Now that you say something, it does look a little disheveled." Dipping his head, he whispered. "As if you were snogging on the rooftop."

Score another blush. If he thought she'd agree, he'd drag her back to the rooftop for a repeat performance. Seeing as how they couldn't, they'd have to find another way to fill the time. "Since we're going to stay," he said, "would you rather eat or dance?"

As if to help his argument along, the deejay began to play a Christmas love song. Susan's arms looped around his neck. "Dance," she said.

Good. Food was overrated.

They did eat eventually and mingle, as well. He wished Susan could have seen herself from his vantage point. She was charming and funny as she moved from group to group. Not a shred of shrewishness or unlikability in sight. "For a wallflower, you are amazingly charismatic," he told her later, while they were dancing. It was the end of the night, and the deejay was playing the last slow dance of the evening, or rather the fifth last slow dance as Lewis had slipped him a few bills to keep the songs coming.

"If I was, it's because I had a star on my shoulder," Susan replied. She had her cheek against his lapel and her arms wrapped around his waist. They probably looked more like they were hugging than dancing. "You make me feel charismatic."

Nonsense. She was her own star. She didn't need him to be anything. Someday she'd realize that.

"People are leaving. I don't suppose Linus will release you from duty."

"Afraid not," she replied. "Even if I weren't in the doghouse, I'm stuck here until the last employee leaves. Turns out that's the tradition. Something Linus said I'd know if I hadn't skipped out all the time."

"Any way we can convince all the employees to leave now? Pull a fire alarm or something?" He was dying to get her home so he could peel off that dress and share his good news. In that order.

"I wish." Letting out a long sigh, Susan burrowed closer. "Why don't you just tell me your news now? You know you're dying to, and I'm dying to hear it."

"Won't be as fun though." Still, she was right about him being eager to tell her. "Let's sit down though." It was the kind of news best told face-to-face.

"Do you remember when Graham Montclark said he would vouch for my character if necessary?" he asked once they'd settled in at a nearby cocktail table. Susan nodded. "Turns out, he went ahead and vouched anyway."

"I don't understand."

"I got a call this morning from his network asking me to come in for a meeting. They've decided to add a new face to their game-coverage team and they think I'm the right face."

Slowly, Susan's eyes widened as the meaning of his news settled over her. "Are you saying…?"

"It worked." Man, but it felt amazing to finally say the words out loud. "Our crazy plan worked!"

CHAPTER TEN

SUSAN LET HIS NEWS sink in. Lewis was going back to football. He would feel like he had a home again. "That's…" It was a good thing. It was what he wanted. Rising from her chair, she threw her arms around his neck. "I'm so happy for you," she whispered. Lewis was getting his dream.

Meaning hers was over. With his mission accomplished, there was no more reason for their arrangement. Stupid her, telling him the affair could end with their agreement. Had she really thought she could sleep with Lewis and escape unscathed?

"I couldn't have done it without you," he said. "You believed in me."

"No, it was all you. You're the one who did the work and actually changed. All I did was help get the word out."

And now he didn't need her. She blinked away the lump in her throat.

"Look at me. I'm so happy, I'm getting teary," she said wiping her eye. "We need to celebrate."

"That's kind of the reason I wanted to go home."

Her heart twisted at the words. Wouldn't be too many more times she'd hear him say them. Not now that he no longer needed her. "How about we settle for a toast in the meantime? Champagne for me, water for you. I'll go get it."

Immediately he reached for her arm. "You don't have to do that."

"I want to." She needed the moment to shake the thoughts from her head. "This is your celebration. You sit and let me wait on you."

Pushing her lips into a smile, she scurried to the bar, choosing the one outside the ballroom so she could duck into the powder room and wipe her nose. Someday she'd get through an event without having to hide in the bathroom at some point, but not tonight.

And, because the world really wanted to mock her, Ginger and Courtney were seated along with a few of the PAs at the table nearest the door to the restroom. Both of them shot a trademark smirk in her direction as she approached.

Whatever. She didn't have time for them.

That is, until she was almost through the door. That's when she heard Courtney.

"Fake," she said.

Susan stopped in her tracks. Stepping behind the door, she leaned her ear close to the crack to listen, the nerves in her stomach doing a tap dance.

It was probably nothing.

"...heard her clear as day," Courtney said. "She told Linus that the whole romance was a scam to get him some publicity."

"You mean they aren't an item?" someone asked. "What about those pictures of them kissing?"

"Totally for the camera," Courtney said.

Susan's stomach felt like it had been punched. No wonder Courtney had smirked at her. She'd overheard everything. The witch had probably spent the whole party spreading the story to anyone who would listen.

What was she going to do? Lewis was going to kill her.

She found a different entrance and rushed back to the table. Lewis frowned upon seeing her. "Where's your champagne? Did they cut you off?"

The ballroom wasn't the proper place for

this discussion. There were too many people still gathered at the tables nearby. If they hadn't heard the story, she didn't want them to overhear anything now.

"You know what?" she said. "Screw Linus. Let's go home and celebrate properly."

Under any other circumstance, the way Lewis's brown eyes lit up would have made her knees weak. "Are you sure?" he asked.

"Definitely." They'd talk when they got to her place.

As it turned out, Lewis gave the driver directions for his place. That was fine. They could talk there, as well. She chewed the inside of her mouth while he pressed the combination on his apartment lock. It would be fine, she realized. Courtney could spread the rumor all over the company if she wanted. She and Lewis could always debunk it. Who would they believe—a known company gossip or the two of them? And even if they didn't believe her and Lewis, it was only Collier's. Wasn't like anybody who worked there was going to alert the press.

Yeah, she would tell Lewis and it would be fine.

The first time she saw Lewis's apartment, she'd joked that it looked like a set for a bachelor-life reality show. Lots of chrome and retro-style furniture and a hot tub with a view to rival the London Eye. She thought that again as she dropped her wrap on the glass dining room table.

Lewis stepped up behind her, his large hands curling around her shoulders. "Finally," he murmured. "I've been waiting all night to get you back here."

Preoccupied or not, Susan's eyes still rolled back at the growl in his throat. "Lewis, there's something I need to…"

His lips found the curve of her neck and those were the last words she said on the subject. It could wait until morning, she thought as her head fell back against his shoulder. There was still plenty of time to nip the gossip in the bud.

It was snowing when Lewis woke up. Big slow-falling flakes like the kind in TV movies. They blanketed the trees and parked cars with white. He pulled a nylon jacket over his running shirt and grabbed a knit cap. Running in the snow had always been a favorite pastime, even as a kid. While his teammates complained and moaned about working out in unseasonable weather, he embraced it. There was something strangely invigorating about cutting through the snowflakes. Besides, he could always count on the snow to clear his muddled head.

This morning, his head was clear as a bell, but he had too much energy to sit still. Susan was still asleep, wrapped up in the covers. He smiled and for a second he considered waking her up instead of running. But there would be plenty of time later. It was going to take a lot more than a run to burn off his high.

Other than the Youth Ambassador Event, Lewis couldn't remember the last time he'd felt this good about life. All the pieces of his goals were coming together. He was back in sports where he belonged, back on a team. And maybe now that he was back on top, he could convince Susan to continue their arrangement a little while longer.

Being with her was as close to belonging as a man could get.

After a few laps around the park, he made a quick stop for scones and a copy of the *Looking Glass*. The vendor sold *Personal Magazine* as well so he grabbed a copy of that too since Susan and he were scheduled to do that interview with the magazine later in the week. He was half tempted to cancel since the article wasn't needed. On the other hand, he liked the idea of Susan gracing the pages of a national magazine. Letting the whole country see more of her uniqueness.

That reminded him, he'd have to find a place for a Christmas tree. When he was done "waking up" Susan, he would ask her what she wanted to do for decorations.

The bed was empty when he unlocked the door. Susan was in the bathroom. It was that last loop. He knew he should have cut it short. Oh, well. He'd give her a few moments of privacy, and then join her. The shower wasn't built for two for nothing.

As he kicked off his running shoes, he idly flipped through the paper where he'd dropped it on the kitchen island. It was the usual headlines. The prime minister was fighting with Parliament. One of the royal duchesses had made an appearance in an expensive designer coat. He turned to page six and froze when he saw the headline.

Scam-pagne Lewis? Fans Duped by Publicity Stunt.

What the…? This was not good. Not good at all. This was…

He ran a hand over his mouth. This was a disaster. Quickly, he scanned the article. It detailed how he and Susan had conspired to improve his image and get publicity for Collier's at the same time, even implying that he was paying Susan and that he was the same drunken playboy he'd always been. Half of it wasn't true at all, and that mattered. Once a narrative was cast, it was near impossible to sway public opinion.

This was going to ruin everything. Goodbye new career, new reputation. Men like Montclark would want nothing to do with him now.

Snatching the paper in his fist, he stormed into the bedroom and thrust open the bathroom door. Susan was just stepping out of the shower. Upon his bursting in, she grabbed a towel.

"What the heck, Lewis," she snapped.

"We've got a problem." He held up the paper so she could see the headline.

A curse escaped her lips. Taking the paper, she continued reading as she padded past him into the bedroom. Lewis followed, reaching the bed in time to hear her swear again.

She'd turned pale. "I didn't think it would make the papers," she said in a low voice.

"What are you talking about? Did you know something like this might happen?"

"Not this." She ran a hand through her curls, sending droplets of water across the comforter. "This is my fault," she said. "I told Linus last night and Courtney overheard. I didn't know she was there but at the end of the night I heard her and Ginger telling others. I'm not sure how it got in the paper though. One of the servers or bartenders must have heard her."

"Dammit. Didn't we agree that we couldn't tell *anybody* for this exact reason?"

"I'm sorry."

Sorry wasn't going to change the fact his reputation was ruined. Again. "Why would you tell Linus in the first place?"

"I didn't set out to," she replied. "He was going on about some family-bonding trip and it came out. I didn't know Courtney was there."

"Well, she was," he snapped. "And now all of London knows."

"I'm sorry." Her eyes were wet with tears.

Blowing out a breath, Lewis got up and retrieved a bathrobe from his closet. He couldn't have this conversation with her wrapped in a towel. She looked too vulnerable. The rational part of him knew it was an accident. That she hadn't intentionally set out to ruin their plan, but he wasn't ready to listen yet. Not when everything he wanted was tumbling out of reach. "I need to go for a run," he said.

"But you already went."

He looked down at his damp running clothes. "Another one. I need to clear my head."

"Don't." Her hand landed on his arm. Lewis turned around. His robe was oversize, the sleeves hanging several inches below her fingers. It was worse than seeing her in the towel.

"It's only one article," she said.

"Right now. You saw how the first one spread." By tomorrow they would be dissecting it on the morning talk shows.

The shrill sound of a phone ringing cut through the tension. "Yours," he said.

She rummaged through her bag. "It's Thomas."

He'd heard about the article, no doubt. "You better take it."

"He can wait until we're done talking."

"What more do we have to talk about? The damage is done."

"Not necessarily. We just need to get out ahead of things. We'll tell people it was a vindictive ex-girlfriend or someone with a grudge. If we do it right, we can spin this in our favor."

"How, when it's the truth? We aren't a real couple."

Her lower lip started to quiver. Lewis had to look away.

"We both said it that night in front of your apartment. A casual hookup that doesn't mean anything. We aren't some grand romance."

Why would she want to be with him now anyway? His chance at redemption was done. If he was untouchable before, because of his reputation, surely, he was doubly so now that the papers branded him a fraud.

He couldn't see bouncing back. Not this time. Might as well walk away from Susan too, and end everything in one cut.

"You should go talk to your brother," he said walking away. "Fix what you can."

"What were you thinking?" Thomas asked. With the baby sleeping in the bassinet a few feet away, he kept his voice a whisper. That didn't hide his frustration however. "A phony romance?"

He paced back and forth in front of the ornate giant tree the decorators had installed in

his living room as Susan watched his prog-
ress from the couch. "I knew something was
odd from the start, but Linus convinced me
that you were the real thing. I couldn't believe
when he told me last night. And now this?"

He pointed to the paper that lay on the
cushion next to her.

"That," Susan replied, "is not my fault.
Gossip columnists have spies everywhere.
All it takes for things to spiral out of control
is for someone to overhear a single conversation."

"If I find out one of my employees leaked
the information, they're going to be out the
door."

Susan kept quiet. As satisfying as it would
be to toss Courtney and Ginger under the bus,
she wouldn't. If they were guilty, Thomas
would find out easily enough and deal with
the problem. Susan didn't need to add fuel to
the fire without proof.

"What did you and Lewis think you were
going to gain by doing this?" The question
came from Rosalind who, until she spoke,
had been sitting quietly next to the bassinet
watching.

"A new reputation," Susan replied. Still
pacing, Thomas let out a loud scoff. "He re-

ally is a different person," she said. "About as far from Champagne Lewis as you can get. Only no one would believe him. Everyone was waiting for him to slip up."

"So to prove he was reliable, he decided to lie to the press. Fabulous." Her brother rolled his eyes.

"It's called a contractual relationship and it's done all the time by actors and athletes. Especially if they need a socially acceptable partner or have a project to promote. I wouldn't be surprised if my mother's had one."

"Oh, by all means, let's copy your mother's bad example."

"Thomas," Rosalind admonished.

"It's all right," Susan told her. Belinda certainly wasn't the best role model. "My point is, this wasn't some nutty scheme Lewis dreamed up. There's precedence."

"Let us get this straight," said Rosalind calmly. "You're saying that Lewis needed to be seen with someone like you to look respectable?"

"Precisely. I'm the complete opposite of the women people picture him dating. The idea was that being seen with me would prove he was no longer the same man. And he's not."

Didn't matter if he'd broken her heart a half hour ago. She would defend Lewis's character until the end.

"He needed an image makeover and this seemed like the best and most subtle way to do it," she said. "It almost worked too. Graham Montclark vouched for him to the network. They were talking about giving him a broadcast job."

Until this morning. Susan couldn't imagine Lewis's despair. To be so close to what you wanted only to have it taken away.

Actually she could imagine. She wanted to curl up and cry her broken heart out for a week. Only thing stopping her was maintaining a front for Thomas's inquisition.

Thing was, she couldn't blame her brother for being angry.

"All right." He sat down in a chair across from her. "I get what Lewis was trying to do. Why would you agree though? What could you possibly be getting? And don't say publicity for the company, because we both know that couldn't have been your main driver."

She shrugged. "Maybe I needed an image makeover too."

"What?" Thomas and Rosalind spoke together.

"Come on, there's no need to act all shocked," she said. "We all know I'm the unloved elf of the Collier family."

"The what?" Thomas asked.

"The one who doesn't fit in and who everyone would rather just went away."

"No one wants you to go away," Thomas said. "You're our sister."

"Half sister," she reminded him. "And please, I know I drive everyone crazy. People at the company only tolerate me *because* I'm your sister."

"I don't believe that," Thomas said. "Linus told me last night that you were the belle of the ball."

"Because I had Lewis with me. When I'm with Lewis I feel different. Likable." Wanted.

"Is that why you agreed to the idea?" Rosalind asked.

She nodded. "Yes. Kind of." Close enough anyway. "I wanted people to see me as more than I am. I thought if people think someone like Lewis could fall for me, they would see there's something likable about me after all and I wouldn't…"

"Wouldn't what?" Thomas asked. For the first time since the conversation began, his voice was gentle. The kindness threatened to dislodge her withheld tears.

"Be the loser outsider anymore."

"What are you talking about? You're not an outsider." Thomas said. "You're my sister."

"Half sister," she corrected again.

"Whatever," he replied. "It's not your fault who your mother is."

"A woman who took off and stuck you with me," Susan added.

He waved off the comment. "Linus and I always figured you dodged a bullet when that happened. You call yourself a loser outsider now. Imagine the damage if she'd stuck around and raised you. Imagine the kinds of issues you might have had to face."

Susan didn't know how to respond. He was right; she would have been worse off. The three of them sat quietly for a few minutes, listening to the baby's gentle sleeping noises.

Eventually, Thomas leaned forward, resting his forearms on his knees. "Linus told me last night he didn't believe you. About the relationship being fake. He said you two looked pretty into each other and he thinks you only said it because you wanted to get him off your back."

He'd whispered something similar to her when they were on the dais. *You don't look like you're faking to me.*

"That was wishful thinking on his part." On her part too. "We had to put on a show in order to make people think the relationship was the real deal."

"By loving it up on the roof?" Susan looked up from her lap. "He told me on the phone."

"I've got to say, that doesn't sound too fake to me," Rosalind said.

"It was nothing serious. We figured since we were going to spend the month together and were attracted to each other, we might as well enjoy ourselves. We weren't some great romance," she added, quoting Lewis.

"And how'd that arrangement work out for you?" Thomas asked.

Susan didn't answer. Couldn't answer really, without her voice cracking. She studied the wrinkles in last night's dress.

"I'm sorry," her brother said.

"Me too." But hey, for a few glorious weeks, she'd felt special. "I've got no one to blame but myself. The whole point was to go against type, so I knew going in he wasn't going to stick around. Caveat emptor or something like that."

A tear escaped. The first of the day. Swiping it away, she looked over at Thomas. "I never meant for Collier's to get stuck in the middle of this. I'll step away from the company."

"What? Why would you do that?" he asked. "No one is suggesting you step down from anything."

"But the bad publicity. You're going to need to do something."

"It won't be firing my sister. You're a Collier. The company is as much a part of your legacy as it is mine and Linus's. Was I the only one who listened to Grandfather when he brought us to the company museum?"

He crossed the room to sit next to her. "Bottom line is that family is what makes Collier's. We've survived four hundred years. We'll survive a few weeks of tabloid coverage. Might even help. We're getting a lot of free advertising."

Susan gave up trying to rein in the tears. Letting them escape, she hugged her brother tight. "Thank you." It was the first time she'd ever truly felt like a Collier.

"You're welcome. And you're not an unloved elf. Just an annoying one."

Annoying, she'd take.

"Now," Thomas stood up and smoothed the

front of his sweater. "I'm going to call the office and see what kind of statement they're putting out before Rosalind and I go Christmas shopping."

As she watched her brother head upstairs to his office, Susan felt moderately better. At least things were okay with her family.

Family. She repeated the word to herself with a sense of shame. Lewis had tried to tell her that she mattered to her brothers, but she hadn't believed him. Turned out Lewis was right. Someday she'd have to thank him. If she ever saw him again.

Baby Noel was starting to fuss in his bassinet. Must be nearly feeding time.

"I'm sorry. I disrupted your morning," she said to Rosalind, rising to leave. "I'll get out of your way."

"Hold it right there, unloved elf." Wearing a very deliberate expression, her sister-in-law rose from her chair. "It's high time you got a dose of the truth."

CHAPTER ELEVEN

"Do you remember last Christmas when you read me the riot act?" Rosalind asked. "You told me I was as much to blame for my problems as Thomas?"

"Of course, I remember."

"You said things no one else was willing to say. Things that were uncomfortable for me to hear."

"Someone had to."

"You're right. Someone did," Rosalind said. "And if you hadn't, we might never have had our little Christmas miracle here." She paused to scoop up the baby and cradle him. "That is why I'm going to return the favor."

Susan's skin was starting to twitch again. "How so?"

"I'm going to tell you some truths," Rosalind said. "Starting with the fact that for someone who's so obsessed with psychology, you suck at self-awareness."

Susan felt as though she had been slapped. "Excuse me?"

"You heard me," Rosalind said. "Do you honestly believe you're some ugly little lump that no one likes? Give me a break. If that's the case then why were you invited to a half-dozen weddings this year?"

"I don't know. Maybe because I'm the boss?"

"Correction. My husband is the boss and Thomas wasn't invited to half as many."

He wasn't? Susan always assumed he didn't attend because he'd scaled back his business commitments since their reconciliation. "Probably because they know he's been pre-occupied, and figured they'd invite the one most likely to attend."

"What about Linus? Did they figure he was too busy, as well?"

"I…" She couldn't answer that. Everyone loved Linus. "He's been distracted lately too."

"So these people knew Thomas and Linus wouldn't attend their weddings, but figured you would and that was why you got an invitation?" Rosalind folded her arms. "Do you hear yourself?"

"If you're going to put it like that, of course it's going to sound ludicrous," Susan said.

"How would you put it then?"

Susan opened her mouth only to shut it again. She wasn't sure. "Company social invitations don't mean anything. There could be any number of reasons why I drew the short straw."

"And what about last night? Linus said you mingled with the best of them."

She'd already told them the reason. Lewis had been by her side. "Mingling is easy when you're dating a celebrity. I've been a rock star all month. Everyone wanted to chat."

"Or maybe," Rosalind said, "it was that for once, you were willing to chat back."

Susan frowned. What did that mean?

"I've seen you at Collier's functions," her sister-in-law went on. "You tuck yourself in the corner and act all aloof. When someone comes up to talk to you, you're fine, but otherwise you pull yourself away. You're the one being antisocial, not them."

"That's not true."

Rosalind arched her brow. "Really?"

All right, maybe she did stand off to the side, but it was only as a matter of self-preservation. Pretend you're not hurting, and you won't.

"You would too if your coworkers thought you were a shrew."

"What?"

At the sight of her sister-in-law's shocked expression, Susan felt a twinge of satisfaction. "*Shrewsan*. That's my nickname at work."

"Who calls you that?"

"Everyone."

"Seriously."

"Well, almost everyone," Susan said, feeling defensive now. "Courtney and Ginger…" She paused. Come to think of it, they were the only two people she'd heard use the term. She only assumed the rest of the company did, as well.

Was it possible she was allowing the nasty opinion of two trolls to color her opinion?

No, because her problems had been going on far longer than that. School. University. She'd been separated from the world her entire life.

She offered her final argument, daring Rosalind to come up with a counterpoint. "If I'm so damn likable, then why isn't my phone ringing with invitations? Why am I stuck spending weekends alone?"

"Probably because people think you'll say no if asked." Rosalind adjusted the baby on her shoulder. "I've heard you back out of plans with Linus. I'm sure you back out of others."

Like invitations to lunch.

"Look, I get it," her sister-in-law continued. "Thomas told me what your mother is like. But did you ever think that the reason people don't socialize with you is because you don't socialize with them?"

"Why should I?" Susan said. "They're only going to…"

"What?"

"Leave." She didn't need to listen to this. Not today. "I've got a headache," she said, starting for the door.

"How do you know?" Rosalind asked. "How do you know people will leave if you don't give them a chance to stay?"

Was that what she did? Susan sat on the edge of the sofa and thought hard about Rosalind's words. All this time she was protecting herself, was it possible she was being her own worst enemy?

"Lewis left," she whispered.

"He's just upset." Rosalind's voice softened, the way Thomas's had earlier. And like before, Susan felt the tears threatening.

"You're worth a lot more than a fake boyfriend or a casual hookup. You're pretty and you're smart, and if Lewis Matolo didn't appreciate that for anything beyond what you could do for him, then he's the one missing out."

Susan would listen to a lot of things, but disparaging remarks about Lewis weren't on the list. "Lewis is amazing. He's the most amazing man I've ever met. I don't think he even knows how amazing he is. I'm just not in his league."

Rosalind sat next to her. "Yes, you are. You're a Collier. You have four hundred years of legacy behind you. You can be in any league you want."

She didn't know what to say. For the third time in twenty-four hours, she was being told she mattered to the family.

All you really need are a few people who care. That was what Lewis had said. Looked like she had those people.

If only she could make Lewis care for her too. "I think I'm in love with him," she told Rosalind.

Her sister-in-law snaked her free arm around Susan's shoulders. "Then let's hope he smartens up and realizes what he had."

Susan didn't know if that was possible.

Rosalind's lecture stuck with her the rest of the day and into the evening. How appropriate that it would be her sister-in-law who delivered the tough love. Last year at this time, it'd been Susan reminding Rosalind of something similar. As she nursed her glass of wine, she found herself circling a familiar cliché: the pot calling the kettle black.

Looking across the street, she saw most of her neighbors had their Christmas trees lit. One apartment was throwing a party. Seeing the people laughing in the window, she wondered if it was true and her insecurities were her own worst enemy. She'd certainly been wrong about her family. All those years of feeling like a square peg, unwanted and unlike the rest, and it turned out her brothers didn't care what shape she came in.

Of course, that didn't change things with Lewis. All the tough love in the world wouldn't make him want her. She'd laid herself bare and he'd rejected her.

Did he? Or did you hold him at arm's length too?

From the very start, she'd been waiting for their affair to end. Pretending for both their sakes that their lovemaking didn't mean anything.

But it did. She loved him. What they shared had been real on her part. She'd never told him though. In fact, she'd pretended she didn't care. She hadn't even invited him to Christmas Eve for crying out loud. How was he supposed to know she cared unless she let him in?

Downing the rest of her wine in one swallow, she grabbed her phone. Lewis's number was on speed dial. Number one. She pressed the button before her courage ran out.

His voice mail answered.

"Hey, Lewis, it's me." She rushed the words as fast as she could. "I know I'm the last person you want to talk with right now, but I wanted to let you know I'm sorry for..."

No, that wasn't what she wanted to say.

"I wanted to let you know that you were the best fake boyfriend around and that I love... loved every minute we spent together. As far as I'm concerned, the relationship was real— very real—and I'm sorry that I ever said anything to Linus. If I could take it back, I would because you deserve nothing but the best. Oh, and Lewis..."

She stopped herself from disconnecting.

"If there's any chance you feel the same or *could* feel the same...please come to Thomas and Roseanne's vow renewal on Christmas Eve. Not because I need a date, but because

I want to see you again and there's nothing I'd like better than to spend the holidays with you. You…you matter to me."

There, she thought with a sniff. No one could say she hadn't made the effort. The rest was up to Lewis.

There was only one thing to do when the going got tough, and that was turn off his phone and belly up to the bar. And, because he was a glutton for punishment, he picked the place where the whole debacle had started. The bar was as empty as it had been a month ago. Emptier. Because a particular brunette wasn't perched on a stool nearby.

"Hey, welcome back."

Just his luck. It was the same bartender.

"Are you here alone or is your girlfriend with you?"

"Haven't you read the papers?" Lewis replied. "She wasn't my girlfriend."

"Could have fooled me. You two looked crazy about each other."

"Goes to show, you can't always believe what you see. Lady was way out of my league."

"Huh."

"What?" Lewis asked. He couldn't believe he was discussing his love life with a bartender. On the other hand, he was in a bar so who else was going to talk with him? It beat staying home and wondering what he was going to do with his life. "If you have an opinion, you might as well go ahead and say it."

The bartender shrugged. "You didn't strike me as someone who hesitates about going after what you want, no matter how out of reach it seems."

"Once upon a time maybe." When reaching meant getting out of a lesser situation. "Unfortunately, just because you want something doesn't mean it'll last." Especially if you didn't belong in the same world. People walk away.

Unless you send them away. Like he had Susan. Why wouldn't he though? He was washed up. His chance at redemption had blown up in his face. Why would Susan want to stick around when she could do so much better?

"Here." The bartender set a bright red drink in front of him. "You look like you could use this."

"What is it?"

"A virgin Christmas Wish. On the house."

Lewis had to laugh. There was a joke in there. He stared at the bubbles rising in the red depths. Susan. The bubbles reminded him of Susan. Oh, how he wished he could fix what he'd messed up.

If wishes were horses, beggars would ride. He remembered someone telling him that as a kid. His first foster mum maybe. The one who was like Susan. Because of course.

"Excuse me. Are you Lewis Matolo?"

Looking up from the glass, Lewis saw a man in a bellman's uniform. "I saw you walk in," the man said.

He was middle-aged, with salt-and-pepper hair and weathered brown skin. "My name is Darcus Alajua," he said. "You met my grandson David at the Youth Ambassador Event."

The man pulled a phone from his jacket pocket to show its wallpaper—a picture of Lewis and a young boy of around eight.

"I remember him," he said. "Speedy little thing. Good footwork."

"I wanted to thank you. Meeting you is all he's talked about for the past week."

"Wow, with Christmas right around the corner, that's a pretty big feat," the bartender remarked.

Lewis was surprised. He remembered praising David's skills a few times, but he hadn't given the boy any additional attention or singled him out in any way that would merit the boy being that impressed.

"I'm glad he enjoyed himself" he said.

"It's more than enjoyed," Darcus said. His eyes dropped to the screen for a moment and grew misty. "David came to live with me a year ago because his mother…my daughter… has some demons. He's been discouraged, feeling sorry for himself. Sports has been the one thing he's enjoyed."

"I know the feeling." He'd been in David's shoes once.

"I know and when you talked about how football saved you, how it helped pull you out of tough times, it lit a fire in him. He's excited about something again."

"I'm glad. You tell him not to give up, and to keep playing. Sports isn't about being a superstar. It's about belonging and being a part of a team and learning to work at what you love."

The older man smiled, the lines on his cheeks fading and his face turning youthful. "I can see why he enjoyed your talk."

"I enjoyed giving it. Being with the kids reminded me of why I fell in love with football to begin with. When you grow up like I did, you need that escape."

"Yes, you do," Darcus said. "That's why it means a lot to the kids when someone like you comes back home."

Comes back home. Was that what he'd done? "Can I see that photo again?" he asked Darcus.

This time he studied David's face. The kid was looking at him like he had hung the moon.

Who else had looked at him like that? Susan.

Lewis handed the phone back with a smile. All his life he'd needed—wanted—a place where he belonged. He thought that place was football. But it wasn't. Athletic stardom had never come close to how he felt when working with those kids. The only thing that made him happier had been when he was holding Susan.

You don't need the spotlight. All you really need are a few people who care.

Susan's smile had felt more like home than any stadium or spotlight ever could. She'd believed in him. Understood him. He hadn't needed the spotlight to win her support.

And he'd sent her away. Since when did he not go after what he wanted? He was Champagne Lewis Matolo, for crying out loud!

He pulled out his wallet. "Do me a favor,

will you?" he asked Darcus. He handed the man a hundred-dollar bill. "You take this and buy David the best football cleats and shin guards money can buy. Tell him his friend Lewis owes him for making him see something very important."

If the company Christmas party had taken place in a winter wonderland, then Thomas and Rosalind's vow renewal was being held in its more glamorous cousin. Her brother had spared no expense in making the Christmas Eve ceremony special, right down to the grand piano he'd had installed in the living room for the occasion.

"I may have gone a little crazy," Thomas admitted as he took Susan's coat along with the bags of Christmas gifts she'd brought for the next morning.

"Rosalind would have been happy renewing our vows in the middle of a field, but Maddie wanted to have a sparkly wedding."

Susan took in the myriad of lights and candles, enough to rival the Kew Gardens display. The regular lighting had been turned off because the decorations provided more than enough illumination.

"Good thing you don't overindulge your daughter," she said.

"Hey, it's Christmas Eve. If you can't go crazy with decorations at the holidays, when can you?" He kissed her cheek. "Merry Christmas. You look lovely."

"Thanks." She'd splurged on an evening gown for the occasion. Silver with sequins. No more hiding herself in the corner. If she was to be a square peg, she was going to own her edges. "I'm afraid I don't feel very lovely though."

"No word from Lewis?"

"Afraid not. We had an interview with *Personal Magazine* scheduled for yesterday, but I got a call from his agent saying the interview was canceled."

No surprise there. For a short while she'd hoped they might go through with the interview to contradict the negative publicity, but apparently not. Like Lewis had pointed out, how did you contradict the truth?

The answer was, you don't. She had this pipe dream that Lewis would use the article to make their casual encounters into something more. But he hadn't.

The fallout from Scam-pagne Gate, as it was lovingly called in the press, was swift and loud. Radio stations all over the UK commented on the story all weekend, which in turn, led to the morning shows holding roundtable discussions about celebrity ethics and England's search for gossip. Lewis was once again a bad boy while her reputation vacillated between coconspirator to besotted victim.

As for Collier's? The company was experiencing their best holiday season in years so either people didn't care that she was involved with Lewis or her being involved with Lewis had helped the company project a saucy, youthful edge. Either way, at least something good had come out of the scheme.

Thomas eyed her with concern. "Are you going to be okay?"

"I feel like a right idiot," she said. She'd fallen for a man when she'd known from the start he wasn't interested in a long-term relationship. "But, I'm not the first person to have had their heart broken. I'll survive." It killed her when she thought of how good she and Lewis could have been together, but she couldn't make him love her. As magical as the past few weeks had been, she deserved more. First and foremost, a man who loved her back.

"Yes, you will," Thomas replied. "Just remember, you're not alone. Your family will always stand by you."

She smiled. "I know." Now.

Perhaps more than one good thing had come out of the debacle.

Rosalind's dose of reality had been hard to hear, but it also gave her a lot to think about. It made Susan take a good look at her behavior over the years. She'd become such an expert at pretending she didn't care about being an outsider, that she failed to see all the times she'd been offered a place inside. She had brothers who cared about her. Sure they were all completely different, and she would never mesh completely with them in a million years. But as Thomas showed the day she and Lewis were outed, when the chips were down, they had her back.

"By the way," Thomas continued, "we found out how the paper got the story. Turns out one of the bartenders at the hotel has a cousin who writes for the *Looking Glass*. She overheard Courtney and Ginger talking at the bar and convinced them to tell her the entire story. She then turned the info over to her cousin."

"Lewis warned me there were spies everywhere. What are you going to do about Ginger and Courtney?"

"Since I don't handle personnel issues anymore, I told senior management that while I wasn't happy with their behavior, I would leave the final decision to them. And you."

"Me?"

"Last time I looked, you were the one who handled human resources," he said. "Plus, you were the victim. If anyone should weigh in with an opinion, it's you."

In other words, Courtney's and Ginger's fates lay in her hands. How circumstances had changed.

Over the week, she'd thought quite a bit about the gossipy twosome. She finally realized that their need to put her down said more about them than it did her. What their reason was for disliking her, Susan didn't know, but that didn't mean their opinion was correct either. In fact, a long talk over coffee with Maria proved their opinion was in the minority. Susan was simply so busy wrapping herself in protective distance that she hadn't noticed.

The question now was how bad a punishment did they deserve? "They didn't purposely leak the story," she said. "More like they were being petty and foolish." On the other hand, their pettiness had caused her and

Lewis a lot of pain. Mostly Lewis. When it came to Susan, the story had only hastened the inevitable.

"Still, they did do damage. It's only by sheer luck Collier's didn't suffer some kind of backlash."

"You can say that again. Personally, I think we should fire them," Thomas said.

"Not me." Susan couldn't believe what she was about to suggest. "I'd rather suspend them for two weeks and give them a stern warning."

Her brother lifted his brows. "Seriously?"

"And I want them to know that I was the one who saved their catty little butts." She wasn't so magnanimous that she didn't want them to owe her.

"Excuse me, you two." Linus stepped into the entryway. "Do you plan to spend the entire evening talking in the entryway or do you plan to attend the party?"

"Merry Christmas to you too." She kissed him on the cheek.

He looked past her shoulder. "Are you here alone?"

"What do you think?"

"Just checking. I need a drinking companion. Come with me to the bar." He tucked her arm into his. "By the way," he said over his shoulder, "your wife wanted me to tell you the maid of honor is getting antsy. She's worried you'll take too long and prevent Santa Claus from coming."

"You know," Susan said as they stepped into the main living room, "Thomas insists that Maddie will be running Collier's someday. I'm beginning to think he's right."

When Thomas said only a few friends and family would be invited, he hadn't been joking. Only a handful of people, a dozen at most, were in the room. Most were gathered by the piano listening to the Christmas carols. Four stockings, fire-engine red, hung from the mantel, the newest one a miniature version of the other three. The magic of it all was like salt poured into her heart, but she forced a smile for her brother's sake. It was just a broken heart. She would survive.

Linus led her to the opposite side of the room where a portable bar had been staged. Susan's eyes nearly popped out of her head.

"You again!" she said. "Are you the only bartender in London this holiday season?" The bartender let out a hearty laugh. "I'm beginning to think so. I was drafted into service by my uncle Chris. He's over there by the guests." He pointed to a portly man with a white beard and red reindeer sweater.

"Well it's good to see you...?" She realized she'd never gotten his name.

"Nick," he replied. "Is your boyfriend with you?"

A little more salt burned her heart. "I'm afraid we aren't together anymore."

"That's too bad. You two made an adorable couple."

She'd thought so too. "Some things don't always work out," she said sadly.

"Or maybe they just take time," he replied. Evidently they taught positive thinking at bartending school. "Can I get you a house special?"

"What's it called this time? Nick likes to name his drinks," she told Linus.

"Yep, and in honor of tonight's special event, we're serving True Love cocktails."

"Fabulous," Linus replied, sounding slightly more enthusiastic than she felt.

"Trust me," Nick told them. "You won't regret the choice."

Their cocktails were barely in hand when the pianist played a loud fanfare. "If you could take your seats," he announced. "Our ceremony is about to begin."

Maddie appeared at the top of the spiral staircase, and as the pianist played a soft classical piece, she began picking her way down the stairs. When she reached the bottom, she scurried to the front of the room to hug her father. She looked adorable. Susan smiled, then looked at the empty seat beside her.

How she wished Lewis were here.

Rosalind was next, looking resplendent in a simple white silk dress. She positively beamed with happiness. No wonder Nick named the drink True Love.

Feeling a little nauseous, Susan took a large sip and watched the ceremony. The look of utter adoration in her brother's eyes made her heart ache. How wonderful must it be to be loved the way Thomas loved Rosalind.

Some day, she told herself. Some day she would have that. At the moment, her heart still wished it were Lewis, but after a week, it was time for her to accept that that wasn't going to happen. Instead, she'd be grateful for the time they'd had.

As she blinked away the dampness from her eyes, she felt someone settle into the empty seat beside her.

"I hope those are tears of joy."

Susan stopped breathing. She was almost

afraid to turn her head. Was that really Lewis sitting beside her? "You... I..."

He put his fingers to his lips. "Shh. There's a wedding going on." A second later, his hand captured hers.

The rest of the ceremony passed in a fog as the only thing Susan could focus on was the man beside her. Did his being there mean he returned her feelings or was he simply fulfilling one last obligation? A tear slipped down her cheek.

"Hey, now," Lewis said as the rest of the group burst into applause. "What's this?" He reached across and fanned her cheek with his thumb, his fingers lingering on her jaw when he finished.

What was he doing, smiling at her like she was the most important person in the world? People were still applauding and congratulating the happy couple, but she needed to know. The moment was too surreal to believe. Or rather, too perfect to believe.

"Come with me," she said. Slipping past the crowd, she led him to the vestibule where they could talk in private. There, partially hidden by a poinsettia tower, she turned to him and finally asked what she'd been dying to ask the entire ceremony. "Why are you here?"

"I got your invitation."

A week ago. She'd left her message a week ago.

She tossed her drink in his face.

"What was that for?" Lewis wiped the True Love from his face.

"Why do you think?" It was an instant reaction and probably over the top, but dammit! "You left me hanging for an entire week!"

"Is everything okay?" she heard Thomas ask.

All five members of her family appeared in the doorway, prepared to stand by her. Even distracted by Lewis, the show of solidarity squeezed her heart.

"Thanks, but I've got this," she told them. "Lewis was just about to explain what the hell he was thinking showing up here after being MIA for a week."

"I was trying for a romantic gesture."

"You call leaving me hanging romantic?"

"Don't be daft. I wanted to call you back as soon as I got the message."

Out of nowhere Nick joined the group, brandishing a cloth napkin. Lewis took the cloth and wiped the last of the liquid from his cheeks. "Okay, I *should* have called you back as soon as I got the message, but I was out of town on business. I decided it would be better if I waited until I saw you in person so I could say I love you properly. Clearly I made a mistake."

"Clearly you did… Wait." Did she hear him right? "What did you say?"

"I said I made a mistake."

"No, before that."

Lewis smiled. "I said I love you, Susan Collier."

Before she could say another word, he drew her into a kiss. He tasted like peppermint and True Love.

God bless silly cocktail names.

"I'm the biggest idiot on the planet," he whispered when they parted. He rested his forehead against hers, his eyes shut tight. "I was so afraid of… I spent my entire life certain the only reason anyone would want me was because of what I could do on the field. That if I weren't a star…if I weren't in the spotlight, that people wouldn't care. I wouldn't be good enough for anybody." Pulling back, he opened his eyes to reveal unshed tears. "Especially not for you."

"You are an idiot." Her lips were trembling

so much, the words barely made it out. "I don't care what you do. I never did." The irony of his confession hit her and she started to laugh. "I thought *I* wasn't good enough for *you*."

"Oh, sweetheart, you are so far out of my league. I consider myself lucky that you would ever give me the time of day."

"We're both idiots," she said. Letting their insecurities keep them from happiness. "I love you, Lewis Matolo."

He brushed her cheek. "I love you too, Susan Collier."

They were the three most beautiful words she'd ever heard.

"My last grand gesture didn't go right, but maybe this one will," he said. "I know we both have a lot of issues to work out, and I can't promise what the future is going to hold for us. But I'd like to find out."

There was a gasp from the room as he dropped to one knee. "Therefore, in front of your friends and family, I'm asking if you'll... date me. For real."

"Yes," she replied, wiping the tears from her cheeks. "I would be honored to be your real girlfriend."

"Daddy, are we having another wedding?" Maddie called out.

"Maybe someday," Susan replied, her heart giving a leap at the smile her answer brought to Lewis's face. "Right now, I think I'll focus on having a very merry Christmas."

Lewis Matolo: How a Fake Relationship Brought Me Love

It doesn't take a genius to see that Champagne Lewis is happy with life. Once the king of London nightlife, he's content these days enjoying a cup of tea and babysitting his girlfriend's niece and nephew.

"I love kids," Matolo says. "They remind you of what's important."

It's that love of children that led the star of *Football Tonight* to establish the Matolo Children's Foundation, which aims to help underprivileged and foster children develop leadership skills through sports. His partner in the venture is his girlfriend, Susan Collier.

"To think," he says, "it all started with a fake relationship..."

Susan stopped reading and tucked her copy of *Personal Magazine* under her arm. "It's brilliant. I told you we could spin this into something positive."

"Yes, you did, and it only took twelve months," Lewis replied. He laughed when she gave him a playful smack.

Hard to believe a year had passed since that horrible night they'd met, which in retrospect had turned out to be the best night of her life. It'd given birth to the best twelve months she'd ever had. Both she and Lewis were making an effort to work through their insecurities. Taking Rosalind's advice, she'd begun trying to be less standoffish and to be open to people. As a result, they were heading to the Regis to help their friends Maria and Hank celebrate their wedding anniversary.

Meanwhile it turned out Lewis hadn't blown his shot after all. The network loved Lewis's new notoriety. The executives thought he brought an extra edge to the broadcast.

"It's too bad the article's going to be out of date soon," Lewis said. "I've already given the network my notice." He'd decided the joy he felt working with kids was far more rewarding than broadcasting.

"I'm sure the world will forgive you," Susan said. "It's not like you left to chase wine and women. You didn't, right?"

"No way, luv. I'm a one-woman man these days."

Susan smiled. The best part of the year had been making their journeys together. Lately they'd even started talking about merging those journeys into one shared life, and if the little square box she'd accidently found in Lewis's drawer was any indication, that merger was right around the corner. Two odd peas no longer unwanted and alone.

Just as they reached the hotel, the first snowflakes of the season began to fall. "Looks like the Christmas season has officially started," Susan remarked. "They'll be playing carols on the radio next."

"A little early Christmas isn't so bad," Lewis replied. "Means the pop-up bars will be setting up shop."

"That's true." Hard to hate those when it was a pop-up bar that brought them together. "Do you think the same bar is here this year? We could stop in and say hello to Nick."

"We could see."

They walked up the stairs to the mezzanine, expecting to find the temporary structure. Unfortunately, when they reached the top step, the space was empty. There was nothing but a pair of high-back chairs and a table with a small Christmas tree.

"Sorry, luv," said Lewis. "Looks like we're out of luck."

No, she wasn't. Her luck was only beginning.

"That's all right," she told him. "I've already got my Christmas wish."

* * * * *

*If you enjoyed this story,
check out these other great reads
from Barbara Wallace*

One Night in Provence
Their Christmas Miracle
Christmas with Her Millionaire Boss
Winter Wedding for the Prince

All available now!